Daddy's Boys

Written by:
Jeremiah Reynolds

Cadmus Publishing
www.cadmuspublishing.com

Published by Cadmus Publishing
www.cadmuspublishing.com

ISBN: 978-1-63751-066-7

Acknowledgements

Please embrace my loves and thank you's to all that crossed my mind as I write this short story. You were my inspiration, to put thoughts on paper and make something of myself with one story that may change my life and the lives of others around me. I just want to show others it is nothing we cannot do with faith and hope. Also the strength to move forward no matter what life throws your direction.

As I spent long nights in a cage forced to face my wrong in life I have learned to embrace my pain and turn it to ones joy. No need to focus on things we do not have control over but use our powers to overcome all things. With the love and support of so many (Y'all know who you are). Thanks for helping me become the man I was raised to be and not give up or turn your backs on me! That means the world to me so forward that I put your name right here on my first page because without you all there would be no me, even my haters. God bless you all I'm still standing, still doing things I never imagined. Even from prison life is good we just got to live it!! Much love far most to my number one lady Mama Jackie, my Queens Tasia, Shanna, Temeshia, my boys Jamiron, Jakiron, and J-Jr., my nephews, nieces, uncles, and cousins. It is for us I do it all my heart bleeds for you!! To my people who rode with me even while I was out of sight out of mind. This goes out to you. Heads up, chest out is the only way Marvin, Brice, D.E., Cobo, Tamara, Reva, Jason, Wilma, P.A.T, A.K.A. Fat Daddy, B-Loc, 4-D, Spoon, The Whole W. U. C. Click, Quincy, D-nice, Shanda, Cook, Meshia, Brittany, Steph, Ebony, Clark, Tootie, Much love and respect. I'm still pushing! South Park is my playground we will rise!! If you were down and I missed you forgive me, it's just so much that I would need a book alone just for that, Shynet, I will not forget you. Keep God first. Elnora is my strongest muscle and I'm going to push till we are one of the great Reynolds style! To all that spend your money to help me provide for my kids I will never forget you. My heart is with you. One day I will give back to you because when I make it we all will. Ayanna, kiss Sunshine and let her know there is no stopping a king. All my fake friends, hey all I can say is it's my fault, I kept it too real. Keep doing your thing though like 2-pac. I'm not mad at you Crack-C, Jason P, y'all tried to show us the right way just know we listened. But most of all God is the King no matter what!!

Like I said, if I missed you and you know you ride with me right or wrong I want you to know it is not intentional so forgive me for that I'm out. Dreams will come true as long as you try.

Tamesha this is for us!! We got this sis!!

RIP Slim, Jake, Tonie, Baby-T, Mike G. Mike G. Spot, Elnora, Tasia, Tony-T, Gator, D-Hoova. Can't leave y'all out, let God know I'm trying. Enjoy the short story and keep hope alive. Black Lives Do Matter.

I'm out,

Jeremiah Reynolds Sr.

Free my boys on lock in them cells stay strong only time will tell young Trap.

CONTENTS

CHAPTER 1

Blood is blood no matter how it spills . . .

Damn man, why you got to push shit to the limit all the times? I can't change what's done. I mean long story short you pushed me out and shit happens, none of it was planned. I mean damn it hurt me to tell you, but the man in me won't let me deny what's mine. . . all I'm asking you to do is stick this one out with me. Let's just make a way trew it all for the sake of our son. We don't need to put our boy trew no more than he's been trew already, Ma. Why don't you just unpack and work it out with me. We gonna figure some things out just give it time . . .

Five years later and I still ain't heard from K. See me and Kay started off young pups in over our heads full of love no doubt. But real short on guidance. When it came to relations, let alone raising a family as a man, I take full blame for all the wrongs that I had brought my family's way, but what do you expect from a fifteen-year-old boy playing man. Shit, truth be told, I just had got my lil piece wet the summer before, I mean after that couldn't no one tell me nothing. I wasn't thinking on the ends and outs of it all or what a true relationship means. I was young and having fun. Hey, but at least I tried. I can't take nothing away from Kay though for the most part she stay down with my bull shit and my cheating ways and if I knew what I know now truth is I would do a lot of things more different.

As you can imagine how can I say this much . . . plain as day I fucked up. Graduation has come and life has got real. Me and Kay, we still going strong seventeen going on eighteen and I must admit I had never thought I would see this day. The day me, Big Jay, will walk across a stage, hold up, let me punch myself right quick, cuz I still can't believe it's true and on time Class of 2003, yea! That's going to look good on my ma's wall right. Shit it's going to look good anywhere. Saying I started four years of high school in the ninth grade! Tell me, how you do that in my master P Voice. No but for real my day here I'm on my way to go take my grad pics. Know I got to stunt hard four years of high school and I went got it all in one semester. Shit who's the damn fool now. Say bae you need anything? Kay sitting over there looking all sexy and stuff like a thanksgiving turkey ready to be eaten up, oh yea. My girl, Kay, she eight months pregnant with our first son. We stay with my mom's. her people put her out when they found out she was pregnant and keeping it. Not being mean, just more of letting us be together since we seem so much in love, and I'd be a lie if I acted like everything was okey dokey cuz that's far from it. Just imagine what we been trew in two full years of high school. Yep, you guessed it, I cheated. I ain't come home a lot. I'm playing in them streets, but Kay still ride for a nigga though. I mean at about fourteen drugs became a way of life for me. I sold my first stone and was hooked ever since. See money wasn't much of a problem, but what to do with it was. Instead of making investments, shit, I just bought a big ego. My way or the highway, shit shame on me. Little did I know the same things that will make you smile will be the things that will make you cry!

What you mean get him shit? You get him. I been at work all damn day. You been here with him all this time. Pick him up and feed him shit. Let me get right fresh off work smelling like onions and shit you know this Mc-Donalds shit ain't for me. Give a nigga credit. I'm trying to man up push the clock and come home, but soon as I walk trew the door. It's get ya son like he become all mines or something. Nigga, shut the fuck up, you ain't the only one go to work around here and just like you smell like onions. Nigga, me to homeboy I do the same shit you do when you get off. I go in so don't tell me nothing about acting like he ain't mine or no shit cuz I put in just as much work as you do with him and on the clock, so nigga fuck you and get ya son. Yep, that's how it is now. Sometimes I wonder where we went wrong when it was school and no child I couldn't buy an argument, now it no school and trying to do right with my family and my new baby boy. Shit go crazy any given second. Like everything an argument. Its cold outside nigga, fuck — the weather, yo son need some new shoes, and his milk low. Damn Bae, my shit hard like a ten-buck roll of quarters so nigga you better go somewhere else with all that nigga. I got to go to work boy, fuck you. I mean everything turn in to the same shit and truth is I can't tell you where it all comes from cuz when we was in school no kid, man, I fucked up every night just left a broad house come home it was hey bae, you hungry. Hey, bae, you want some head. Sometime I feel she use my boy as a trap knowing I'm not gone go as fast or stay out no more. It's a cold thought, but what else do I come up with? Fuck it. Let me just take Baby-J and go in the back room with my lil nigga and we gone jam out while pops get so fresh and so clean fuck some head anyway, shit, turn me weak every time any ways! Kay just don't know man I'm bout tired of this do right. Since I got this job I can barely buy me a pair of shoes. Now I mean our son good no doubt, plus Kay lil bread she makes she share with me, but I don't like asking baby for shit. I mean like I said, since lil money been easy.

Say Kay, let's go take some pics this weekend me, you, and Baby-J. yea, that's what's going on we just need to do more shit together fresh out of high school with a child and work all the time. I see where the frustration comes from shit we don't got time to fuck shit all we did is fight. What about fight and fuck. I'm just saying. Look, nigga, I get off at 11:00 pm tonight don't be all late and shit, Jay, I'm not playing with you, don't have me standing outside waiting on your slow ass and don't have my baby around no hoes, cuz you gone make me kill you nigga. I ain't playing with you! "Man shut up and get the fuck out Burger Flippin ass ain't no body gone be with no hoes that shit happen one time with you and Jen. You ain't let that shit go yet."

What you mean let it go yet nigga better be lucky you still alive. Had my son with that bitch. Let me go in to work fo I get mad all over again. Sorry ass nigga. Yea, yea - I love you too with yo sexy ass. Don't hit me on my ass. I'm not playing 11:00 pm, not 11:30 mother fucker. Stop talking like that in front our son. He might pick up on your ways. Filthy mouth lil girl and bring me a McFlurry with cookies. When I come get you. We about to hit the mall and get some shit to take pics in. You know them hoes gone be boppin on a nigga with my Boss player right on side me. Nigga, play with me if you want. Matter of fact lets go drive off. I'm gone call in we gone go to the mall together girl. No girl, get back out and go to work fo them people fire yo ass.

You know I'm just bull shittin with you, you worry about that so much. But tell a nigga no when I ask for some of my pussy tell me do that add up in any way? If you fuck me good then we wouldn't even talk about other hoes all the time now get out. See ya mean ass .

At 12:00, Nigga what? I'm just playing 11:00 bla bla bla
I know I know say answer me this before you go bae
(what)? you got some draws on? (Lol)

CHAPTER 2

Yea look lil man it's me and you in this Bitch Fuck all that Back seat shit. Let me fix ya car seat on the passenger side so you can see the world from a boss point of view. You gone be just like me we gone run this shit together. We gone ball on them and crawl on them. I'm gone give you the game one-on-one, so no body can't tell you shit different. The world is ours and everything in it. Every time I talk to Baby-J like that he just laugh. I don't care what nobody say them kids know what's going on right son? We bout to hit this mall get us some new fresh shit stunt on a few bops and do us for the rest of the day. You dig nigga. If I get some head don't tell on me. Three-thirty in the evening we pull up to the mall as usual that motherfuck-er stay packed truth be told. This my most favorite shit to do. Hit the mall with my lil nigga. It never fails hoes go crazy every time they see us a young black man with his pride and joy instead of one pair of Jays it's two or four, two for me and two fo Baby-J. That's the way it got to be. Me and my lil nigga who gone stop us?

Hey Jay, that's you and my baby I heard from right over my left shoulder. I knew the voice, but I looked back to be sho just like I thought. It was Jen and some bad ass lil broads she had with her. All four of them looked like dolls so you know I had to turn the charm on. Sup Ma what's good with you. long time no see right? Yea nigga why is that kay got you shook or something you don't even call my phone no more daddy. Come on ma you know we don't bring up our kids parents when we talk is all about us, so I'm gone excuse you for the slip up cuz we got company. Matter of fact how you ladys doing. Hey Jay, the other three said. One looked at my son like she wanted to kid nap my nigga. The other, looking me eye to eye for way much too long to consider normal while the other adjusted her lip gloss on her lips in a slow manner. Shit nothing much actually glad to see y'all cuz I need a lady opinion. I can't choose between the black and red ones or the white, red, and blue foes for me and Baby -J. I need a woman's eye with this one cuz they got the hat and a bad fit for Baby Jay with the black and red ones buy they don't got the fit for me. But with the red, white, and blue ones they got plenty options for me and him. So what I'm asking is if y'all got time can y'all take my boy and pick the best shit for him the type of shit you would wish your own child could have regardless of the price and also the type of shit that's gone make all the lil baby bopps flip they stroller to get to Baby J. They all laughed but went straight to work like that was the moment they been waiting on truth be told. I love for a woman to pick my clothes just not dress me. Most ladies known what the ladies like so I learned that you can never go wrong with the Lady choice.

While all three of them was off with baby – J me and Jen talked on the low for a bit while she look for some shit she thought would look good on me. Say ma wat's good though what you and ya girls up to tonight. Where y'all going when y'all leave the mall? We all going back to my home girl apt. She just came down from a small town called P.A. and we been real tight. She likes me. We play around but we ain't did much serious shit yet unless you wanna show us how that type stuff go? Now you know that push a nigga over the top I told Kay the last time she caught me and Jen together that I was gone dead that shit. I mean I'm not trying to loose my home buy look at what's at hand. Fist one straight shot good head good sex and on top of that offering something new on the side at the same damn time. Now my mind telling me to run but my thoughts say you damn fool what you waiting on. I know if Kay even knew I was talking to Jen that I would kill the whole family things dead.

I look up again at the other three as they look items over and over for the perfect one and the one that's holding Baby Js hand just looks like a movie star to me.

I mean light skin green eye curves on plush looking like a baby Wendy William (LOL). No but for real looking like diamond off players club. Ya feel me. And while I'm looking at her she looks at me and just smile. I can't lie. That's all it took I was hooked. She came over with a red and white and blue and blue jeans 501 pants for my lil man and on top of that the exact same outfit for me just with a different color pattern. That shit was price-less. Hands down crazy thing about it she even had my size right down to the T even the shoes. Now that must be a magic trick or something cuz even my B.M. Don't got me down to a T like this. It left no questions to be asked. It was a no brainer. I just love your son and by the way my name is Jaz. I'm from P.A. I would love to keep him any time you need someone to watch him for you cuz you look like a busy man or just a good dad who brings his son everywhere he goes or is it just y'all lil thing to shop together. She was asking as the other two came back over to us all holding outfits too but in-stead, like Jaz they only had outfits for baby J. Say ladies I've met Mrs. Jaz, me and MS Jen go way back but I feel its rude I don't have a name to put with you pretty ladies now. How cool is that all pretty faces without a name to match unless I can give y'all one if that how y'all would like it. O Yeah and what would that be Mr. Jay the shorter one of the four asked with a smile I would call you Candy cuz that's exactly what you are to my eyes. She laughed and said well candy it is but when you get tired of that my real name is Resha. Well MS Resha's

Candy look like we got it all figured out for you my Lady I said to the last one standing who was darker than the rest of the crew but with a smile that could change any man's mood. I'll call you Sunshine cuz your smile lights all my dark days. She thought on it for a second then she said cool that's what it's gone be cuz I don't like dark days. Plus Jessica seem a lil to white any ways right. We all laughed and just like that Baby-J done it again. Man I swear this lil man a mack and don't even know it. Little to say we went to the cash register, ordered and paid for each item. Wasn't no need to put anything back. Them ladies had taste. They even went in their own pockets and bought shoes, socks, and anything else they thought Baby -J would look good in. Shit who am I to complain as we walked trew the mall me and baby-J looking like true pimps at least to the outsiders looking in. We had a lil time to spare so I offered to by us all food at the food court.

With a lil small talk and a bunch of laughs the ice was broke and I felt like we all knew each other longer than just a few hours. Like they say times fly when you having fun right. We did set up a time for us to meet back up and pick up where we left off back at Jaz apt a lil later on. I can't lie the way all that went so smooth all I could do while I walked out the mall back to the car with more bags than expected and with baby-J right on my side was think of what excuse would I tell Kay when I drop her home from work tonight.

CHAPTER 3

Eight o'clock came fast. I told Jen I would be to their Apt around eight, but you know niggas we won't never be one time. Shitted I left the mall me and Baby-J at bout six and we been on the move every since. Had to stop by my big bro Zilla spot chop game up with fam fucked around poured up a (4) foe, of that Texas tea. Chopped game on some moves that we needed to make. I was all ears when it came to money. Yea I know I said I was doing shit the right way to the public eye though I was; I was working my 9 to 5 six seven days a week sometimes no off days and sometimes more days off than work. That's why I say that money was no guarantee. Money for the life I was used too old Habits die hard but give credit where credit was do. Since I had Baby-J I didn't hustle after 9 p.m., and I never moved with nothing on me. Actually I was down to a hand full of licks. Just people that I came up with was the only ones that could still call. Mamma and Kay couldn't tell no more and that was my main goal with the money I made from the streets. I would stash and hide in my shoe box with my check money. I would help on bills clothes and all on baby J. The American way right? Anyways me and big bro chopped up game I told big bro about this new cat I'd ran across with some much better prices that we were used to. I told big bro to Holla when he wanted to score, and I would set things up. Big bro told me about some new spots that he would open up and we would just bust everything down 50/50 that took about an hour in a half. Baby-J always with me when I go talk business cuz I want baby -J to learn and know all he can from the good side to the bad side. Our only rules was to never bring drugs in front of our kids so no riding with drugs and kids and no sales in front of kids. All else was fair game. We talked numbers. We went by spots. We picked up money but never no drugs that would be done on the one. Jen texted my phone to see if I would still stop by at 8. I replied of course then she asked if I would bring some liquor for them to drink. I don't drink liquor only Tx Tea. So I didn't see no problem watching a house full of ladies go that way. Shit the goose make em loose. You know me I'm up for all that type play. Eight -thirty hit and I was no closer to them or on my way to them than I was at 6.30. So when I read my text from Jen asking if I was standing them up I replied no just was caught up what's the address and apt # again. I'm on my way. She texted back in seam like 20 seconds we on 1400 Brockman Ave Cardinal Sg Apt #04. Cool touch down in ten I said. Dope man. Code be there in 30 minutes case y'all don't know the black man time frame!

First I called my ma and told her I need her to keep a eye on her grandson. It's getting to late for me to have him out and id be back at 11:30 when I picked his mom up from work. After I got the lil fues like always with at $20 bribe. I was pulling up dropping Baby-J to grandma house. My lil nigga cut up when I dropped him off. I swear that boy know what pops be up to cuz long as he's with me he cool. No lie soon as I try to separate all hell breaks loose each time. I left ma spot, grabbed the Cîroc the apple flavor. I heard that tasted good to the ladies and headed to Apt #4 1400 Brockman Ave! when I pulled up it was like a lil after 9 p.m.. That Texas Tea had me filling no regrets. True story. So I texted Jen from outside. She said come in the door open, so I grabbed my piece, tucked it, and locked my doors. You can't never be too sure of things. I tapped the door twice on arrival. Then turned the knob. I could hear the music playing not to loud, just loud enough. So when I walked in shit was crazy all four of the girls was there. Jen, Jaz, Candy, and Sunshine but that's not the part, it's what they all had on that trew me back a few. All of them had on boy shorts, bras, or lingerie that matched. I knew right then I was in the right spot. Crazy thing not a one of them got shy or even budged at the site of me. They just kept at it like I was just part of the crew, so I did what I do best. I made myself at home. I checked each room, bed, closet, bathroom, kitchen. Can't never be to show, then I locked the door and broke out the Cîroc. Man they was playing truth or dare. Having twerk sessions and just doing what girls do. I played it cool though never let them see you sweat. I put a twist on the games they were playing. I dared things never thought of and I poured shot after shot for no true reason. If I asked a question and she got it wrong shot one laugh too long shot one, stumbled when she walked shot, I was in control of a room full of stars what could go wrong!

CHAPTER 4

Times fly when you having a good time! Damn so caught up in the moment I didn't hear my phone go off for the 100th time. I had a filling it was close to 11:00 pm so I went in my pocket to pull my phone out. Shit reality came crashing in on me real fast 11:45 pm, 30 missed calls, 100 new texts. Damn I done fucked up without even fuckin up. Jen could tell something was wrong when she looked up at my face. What's wrong boo? Aint shit I got to slide out real fast forgot some important shit man. Got to get to it ASAP. You gone come back? You know me ma you know I won't be gone long. Keep the party going just got to go grab this lil bread real fast. I lied I don't need no bitch all in my family business. Soon as I cleared the door and got in my car I called Kay's phone. Man the bitch ant even ring all I heard was hello nigga fuck you. I done had enough where my son! I'm leaving yo sorry ass! I mean she ant even take no breath. Say, say, say look here calm down. I'm up the street. I'm just 50 minutes late. Don't trip out I'm coming. The phone hung up. I ant call back cuz soon as I was my phone rang. It was my mom's. Sup ma, hey boy, where you at? On my way to pick up Kay from work. How you gone do that when she right here to pick up Baby-J. this girl crying and all saying you left her at work. What's wrong with you son? Where are you. I'm on my way. Boy, bye, you need to get you shit together. That girl gone leave you and all hell gone start right then. . .

Man, I couldn't make it over to ma house fast enough. When I pulled up everything was calm. Shit I hope she in the room laying down. Was all I could think in my head. Soon as I put the key in the door ma came to the front room. Boy that girl gone, you need to call her and check on ya family. I've tried she won't answer. I thought she was in here mad, no she took Baby-J and left. I instantly got hot all over my body. The thought of my son being gone almost knocked me off my feet. Did she say where she was going? Who she was with, what all she took was all questions that came out before reality struck I fucked up! So I grabbed my phone and I called. No answer. So I texted, no response. Then I got mad and the only thing I could tell myself was fuck her. She just trippen. I'm going back to Jen spot. Kay be back when she cool down. I be fucking up man promise that don't be a nigga intentions. I just hope she calm down and let me explain. Yea, that's how it's gone go. I be fuckin up man. I'm gone have to eat that pussy soon. I'm running out of options.

I texted Jen told her to open the door up I'm pulling up just like clockwork. They were still at it 12:30 am just like it was when I left. So for the moment I got lost in the good times going on around me. Shit was so real I even took a few shots of Cîroc my damn self. Crazy thing somebody should of told me drank ant good with alcohol cuz I turned to a whole nother nigga the freak came out of me and I was on top the world in no time. We played stripped T's and did shit only the mind can think. I was ass necked by the fourth shot and loving every moment. I dared Jen and Jas to kiss each other. Then sunshine and Candy to rub me down in there body lotion. Shit was just what I needed to get past the last hour in a half. Me and Jen went to the back room. She said she needed to talk to me for a sec. lil did I know talking was the last thing we did. She did what she do best and took my whole thing in one gulp! Fucked my head up no lie crazy thing I thought that would be the way the night end until the door slowly opened, and Jaz came in saying some shit about looking for something and she was sorry. Know me I tried my luck told her to come in and show some skills. She went to eating Jen from the back looking me in my eyes the whole time while Jen eat my dick slow and long looking at Jaz bend over like that had me at a lost man. I jumped out of Jens mouth and went stood behind Jas to see that pretty fat pussy from behind. She looked at me and asked do I like what I see? Shit say no more. I went straight to work. I licked my two fingers got them wet and slid them in her slowly then I let my thumb rub her clit until I felt her body start to jerk while she still ate Jen from the back. Then I grabbed her waist and opened her butt cheeks to see that pretty brown round. Then I spit on it and rubbed it in with my thumb and watched that ass start to throb, then I grabbed my manhood and rubbed up and down her walls until my whole dick got wet on it. Then I put it in damn was all I could say. That puss was good wet tight and just right, I went slow so she wouldn't miss a beat with Jen then Jen got up and came to me and laid under me and went to eating Jaz while I was fucking Jaz. Shit had me going crazy. They was doing the fool, so I put my thumb in Jaz ass and fucked her clit and Jen tung even faster then I pulled out and put my shit in Jaz ass. I ant even ask I just did what I want and while I got in motion I massaged Jen breast. Pulled her nipple a bit hard then started fingering her. Shit was crazy. I came out Jaz ass and put my dick in Jens mouth then out her mouth back in Jaz pussy. Man I beat that tongue and pussy hard and fast for the next 30 mins then I bussed a fat as nut all in Jaz. No pull out no nothing the pussy just had my dick on lock plus the drank and the Cîroc ant have me doing no thinking just going in that's all I knew at that moment.

Waking up the next morning around 10:00 am in an unfamiliar surroundings and filling out of place. It took me a few mins to get my head around to where I was looking at the flat screen that stood blank on the bedroom wall over a nice lil stand with a cute lil flower vase decoration on top. On the side, I saw a Sony DVD player, a new Bluetooth speaker and two pictures of Jaz and look like what could be her mom cuz they look so much alike just different ages. Too my left I saw the dresser and mirror with fragrances in a neat spot in the center. Nothing seemed out of place except the bed that I laid on for a young 18-year-old lil mama had her shit laid out. The curtains matched the bed spread and the air was cool and fresh. I could smell food trough the vents like breakfast was being made or been made so I took to the floor and saw my clothes and shoes folded neat and in one spot. I liked that but you know the first thing I did was check my pockets. To my surprise it was all there like Jezzy say! So I reached for my phone remembering the situation with me and Kay. Just a few hours before I checked my call log had a few missed calls from some my bites, but no calls from Kay. So I checked my texts same shit nothing. I figured that Kay be trippin sometimes she know how to blow shit out of proportion but it's cool. I'll just give her, her lil time and space. But I can't lie not knowing where her and my lil man was at was killing me on the inside.

I rose out of bed and stepped into my boxers and went to the restroom that was hooked to the bedroom. I grabbed me a towel and splashed some water in my face, put some toothpaste on the towel and used my finger to brush my tongue and teeth. Hood shit you know how that go then I washed my face and looked myself over in the mirror. Shit I had to piss bad as fuck so I took a lil piss and piss came out everywhere so from that I knew I must have had some good sex last night. Had lil white still dried all on my shit and all. Crazy thing I don't remember much about no sex. I remember everything else until I came to the bedroom but me knowing Jen I know she put her best shit down on me for the night. So I took my boxers back off and stepped right into Jaz shower. She had Bath and Body Works all around the tub and shit everything for a woman. Fuck it I took her lil spung thing on a string and washed my ass dick and ball real good with some Apple Blossom shit. Shit smelled good but I ant want that smell all over my body, so I just hit my main parts and just let the hot water rinse away the rest of last night. I stepped out, dried off and put my same draws back on. I wasn't' trippin long as my ass was clean. I seen some blue magic in her cabinet, so I put a shot in my hair and pressed down on my head with a hot towel to lay my hair back down. I don't use lady's brushes, too much shit be in them for me, but I was cool with the final look when I looked in the mirror once again. Shit, I'm still that nigga I thought as I grabbed my towels and folded them to sit at the foot of Jaz bed. Then I put my cloths back on. I know that I was pose to go take pics tomorrow with my son and Kay but the way shit look that shit look dead, so I'm gone just go to the car and put something on that I bought at the mall the day before. Fuck it, give me another reason to spend more bread on Baby-J anyways.

I stepped out the room a lil after 11:30 all the girls was up and shit sitting on the couch with blankets and food watching movies and shit looking like a big family and all that. What's up Jay, Jaz said ant shit I replied. Then Jen asked you on your way out the door already daddy with a smile. I said no not yet just bout to step to the car and grab a change of clothes right quick. Then I spoke to Sunshine who was just smiling at a nigga I know hoes man Sunshine want me to beat that pussy up all that smiling at a nigga all the time. She catch me at the right time. I'm gone bless her is all I thought in my head. Then I chunked duces at Candy and asked where my food was at cuz the shit she was eating looked damn good over there and just like a choir they all sang at the same time we put you a plate on the stove in foil. We ant wanna wake you up. You was sleep like a newborn then they all laughed like an inside joke went on, that I ant catch I just shrugged it off and headed for the front door to go to my car. Jen came behind me and walked with me to the car making small talk. Well bae what you doing today? You gone bless my game or what she asked? I thought about that for a sec and asked last night wasn't good enough? She poke her lips out and said she ant get her turn. I didn't last long enough? Puzzled I thought to myself I must of bust in her mouth or some shit. Then went to bed so I said the first thing that came to my mind. You know that head gone get me every time then laughed. She hit my shoulder and said that ant all that got you it was all Jaz show last night fucked up part is I can't even remember none of that shit that drank, and Cîroc put me under for a bit. No bullshit! When she said that I instantly got mad. Fuck I beat that pussy up and can't even remember the shit we got to do a retake. I thought for a sec then I said what you mean ma? Jen told me how things went last night and how I left her out to fend for herself so I told her I would bless her before I left and hit the road in a lil bit really still thinking about Jaz while I handed Jen the bag that I chose to wear for the day to carry back in the house. Call it what you want but a motherfucker go to work for her position ya dig?

Back in the house I sat at the table and told Sunshine to grab my food for me in a cool manner just to see how fast I could make her move. Just as you know she jumped straight to it no delays the way shit was going I could get used to this lifestyle real, real fast. When she sat my plate in front of me I touched her hand and told her thank you with that look in my eye that she could not confuse all she did was smiled back and asked me if I wanted some juice. My type of girl, no talk back out of her just smiles and grins!

Shit I couldn't stop there so I asked Candy would she mind pressing my shirt for me. I told her I can't be seen wrinkled in them city streets. Just like clockwork she got straight to it, so I told Jaz to string up my new shoes and that I used her shower already. She said cool and did just as I asked. I started to tell Jen to come give me some head while I eat but I declined the thought it would be a bit much at that time. My goal was to spread my love equal so since Jen and Jaz took last night I would show Candy and Sunshine love today ya fill me. I asked the girls if they smoked, and they all said from time to time and right now would be one of them times. So I called Zille and told bro to drop off a zipp of white rhino at 1400 Cardinal Sq. #4 to hit me when he pulled up. Big Bro pulled up and I sent Candy to the car. I know my bro and I knew Candy would be just his type, so I told her to go grab that from my bro and tell him I'm in the restroom. So I sent you. she did just that while I texted bro and told him to make his self at home that Candy need a real nigga in her life and the ball is in his court. Then I sat back and enjoyed my breakfast.

CHAPTER 5

Twelve thirty slid up on me and it was time for me to make moves and go talk numbers with real important people since I had free time and look like all other plans was delayed so instead of wasting time I'd choose to go make time. So I called Jen to the restroom after id ate and got straight to it you know I had to keep my word. I bent her smooth over no talking no nothing just us looking at each other in the mirror and I ran my dick in her from the back long and strong no games no playing just straight pound game the way I know she like it anyways. Then I bussed all on her ass cheeks and rubbed some on her lips just to be nasty. My bitch is a real fool if you know what I mean then I grabbed a new towel whipped my s hit again kissed my bitch on the neck and told her to stop eating children its unhuman then we both laughed and fixed our shit and walked out the restroom me looking like new money with my fresh shit on that all the girls got ready for me with my old shit in the new bags. Call that the flip flop effect.

When I stepped back out the room all eyes was on me and that's all I needed to see to know 1400 would be my new spot. I told all the ladies if they need anything to hit me up so I wrote my number down and placed it on the icebox that way no one would get jealous or act funny if one would ask for my number. I took all the harm out of it but the ones that play dirty would catch the drift it's a dog-eat-dog world, but a cat taught us how to play.

I made it to my car then checked my phone again still nothing, so I was cool with that I just put all that to the back of my head and focused on business. I cranked the whip and put my 40 in its safe spot just like it go then I dialed Big Red.

Big Red was one of the older cats that I grew up around back in the day. Homie got the game on lock, but you would never know cuz Red don't move like that no more. He work weekdays and off on weekends and do the family thing most of the time. But if you know Big Red then you know them bricks real close by ya fill me. Big Red had told me from day one if I ever wanted to turn on to hit him on the low and we could work something out. Big homie been wanting to see me on I just be on some more shit trying to make everybody else happy and do right type shit but it's all good cuz the people I do fuck with pack fair, and I can hit them up most times to get by on what I need but lately shit ant been all good niggas adding more to the prices and less to the quality in other words just keeping me in their pockets. So I told big Bro Zilla about this new cat, but I never told him who cuz Big Red don't play that way. He don't care how good I say a nigga is he's told me from jump me and me only, but you know I can't cut bro off plus the highway to H-Town is too risky when the same shit right where a nigga sleep. You know how that go cuz. Homie got that change ya life shit fuck 8-ball and zips more like the whole thang or the whole birds nest if you catch my drift. Something he would always tell me from a young nigga Fed money or dead money. I didn't understand then but now that I been playing the game a bit I catch on real fast. Either get real money or get the fuck out the way cuz playing games gone only get you dead so Fed money or dead money is the motto from this day forward.

Yo Big Homie what's good I said after Red picked up his line. Lil Jay what bring you my way he asked it's a sunny day and it look like a good time to step out and play speaking in code yea it does look good. He replied why don't you come stop by and pick ya nephews up and take them with you. I'm at home. Cool be by in 30 I replied knowing we would never talk over the phone so I hung up and put the Lacc in drive knowing that life would be going either one or two ways from here only up for sure and with a family or one deep the other half. Regardless of what it may be I already made the call so it won't be no turning around and truth be told I was cool with either way cuz in my heart I felt that the money would fix everything when I get my bread right Kay gone come home. Quit her job and just take care of Baby Jay like it goes. All I got to do is make the world see my vision and the rest will be just fine so I put my foot on the gas headed to that change ya life shit focus young nigga focus was all I thought as I put my phone down and cranked up some big Pokey Power in the flower power in the flower that's all I ever wanted was the power in the flower.

Pulling up to Red Spot was nothing a regular four bedroom home two car garage, private gate in the back yard. Steel fence in the front. Your average working man's home to the necked eyes and to me I couldn't understand how a nigga with all the money in southeast Texas live so regular? What's the point in making bread if you can't spend it? Was all I thought as I pulled in the driveway behind the ford pickup truck Big Red uses to drive to and from work.

Shutting the lac motor off and grabbing my phone off the charger I opened the door to step out wasn't no need to call or blow no horn Big Red got cameras from one end of the block to the next. So I know he saw me coming and before I turned on his street. Plus cameras on every part of the house and yard even the doorbell. So I just closed my door and walked to the front door where a voice came over the doorbell camera sup Homie. Come on in he said as I reach for the screen door to open the big wood glass door behind it. When I made it in the front room shit took my breath every time man the man got a 92 inch TV across the front wall with marble floors that heat up so you don't need no shoes on at all with the front room set up like a movie theater with a fish aquarium built in the wall on the right side of the front room from wall to wall which behind it is the masters bedroom that you can't even see in just see out trew the fish aquarium, a mural paining of him and the kids in clouds on the roof. Just to name a few things man you would never guess this shit from the outside. Right then and there I knew I had to get that money that change ya lifestyle money. What's up nephew Big Red said to me coming from the back room into the front to greet and shake my hand. Shit nothing much uncle just came to check on you I replied back to him. Man I'm good come on lets go step out back I was putting a new wheel on lil red go-cart. So we went threw the garage that ant even that this motherfucker look like the game room arcade in your local mall or some shit with games everywhere to a pool table to a rock climb wall with glow light and all type shit man made my mouth drool just passing trew. We got to the back yard it only got better a boxing ring in one corner hot tub in the other with a basketball court in the middle shit was playa I can't lie we went sat on the padded deck that was out back hooked to the kitchen where his lady was putting some shit together. He called to her bring me and Jay something to drink Bae and some chips type shit all she said was ok Bae in just a sec. man I wish I could hear that shit from my broad was all I thought. Then I thought about the money that's what that money do all that talk back shit goes out the window. I just cracked a smile. So nephew what's up son he asked getting ready to cut to the chase. I just replied on all the shit that went on since graduation and how I run my family off not taking care of my business. After explaining all that he grabbed me by my head and laughed and said he remembers that type shit, then told me I got to get my family back it's the only way I will thing straight. Then told me a man got to fit the bill so to keep a happy home you got to bring it home which made much sense to me even thought I'd be out making ends meet. Problems still would catch up like shit just wasn't enough and even thought Kay never asked for much the lack of not having was causing the same effect. So after Big Red dropped them jewels on me I took it at face value and knew from then on I was going to put the mash down for the cash and put everything in order. Lil Jay I heard snapping me back to reality, huh, yea what up Unk I said man what kind of numbers you trying to do was the question. He asked me all I could say was astronomical meaning out of space shit. Red laughed you know what's funny Jay he said what I asked you be dead as serious with the shit you say that's why you my lil nigga. Good heart, good head so with that being said Jay say no more and our convo ended. We drank soda, ate chips, and fixed the tire on the go-cart.

In my head I couldn't figure out where our convo ended with the business or where we would pick up all I know was time was passing and we ant really say shit then he said Jay I love you like a son, but I love my family and my lifestyle more. To never bring harm to his doorsteps and that he ant got to where he was being dumb and in a rush but with time and a plan so I just listened and stated Unk I understand, and I guess that sealed the deal cuz he told me that time was getting late, and it would be best to go home and get my head in the game. With that said he stood and hugged me then told me I would never be welcomed back to his home under no circumstances. He would be in touch more often than not and grabbed me by my should to walk me back trew the garage. Confused I was mad and all a bit cuz I ant understand where the fuck it went wrong maybe when I told him about Kay leaving. I knew I shouldn't bring that type shit up now Unk think I'm a young dumb weak nigga was what I thought but I said fucc'it. I'm just gone have to show him too. I been used to getting it out the mud so why stop now I thought. When we made it to the front door he said I love you and bring my nephew back home. That my son is a fine young man. Me all over as if I wasn't already confused the nigga just confused me even more. One minute don't come by then the next he love me and my son. This nigga a trip I thought walking back to my lack all fucked up thinking how much time I'd just wasted. Soon as I stepped in my car there was a note on my steering wheel, so I grabbed it and read it. Note: say neph. always keep ya seat belt on do the speed limit and use your signal. Never know who watching play the game by the rules and you will last long the note read. P.s. look in the glove box so I reached over and opened the glove box and saw a flip phone. Nothing fancy with a note saying this will be our new lifeline. All numbers you need are in your contact list and remember your rights. If your glove compartments locked and your trunk is locked you don't have to open it for no one you will need a warrant for that. So keep ya trunk lock and go straight to where you're going for your future waits for you under your spare tire in the trunk. Drive safe and destroy the notes ASAP Big Unk.

I thought on it all for a second then wondered how did Red do all this when he was with me the whole time and id had my own keys on me. So I put my seat belt on and started my car. On my way to my mom's my only safe spot period in my head so that was the only place I was going. No stops cuz I didn't' know what was in my trunk. But I would soon find out.

CHAPTER 6

Man, I ant lie. That was the most longest ride ever! Getting to ma house was the ;most scarry shit ever man I ant know if I had a dead body in my trunk or what everywhere I look felt like I saw the Laws man not knowing fuck with you more than knowing but not know is what kept me on point the whole ride, so I just played my part all the way to the door. When I got to ma house she was in her room watching TV. Hey ma I said boy come here she stated so I went straight to her where my grandbaby boy she asked ma I don't know Kay ant call or answer where you been all night she asked. Mother Jackie was a trip, but all love come from her. No matter what but one thing she didn't' play was being a dead beat if we made them we had to raise them so I knew she wouldn't let up on me until I knew my son was safe and sound. So I just told her I would call Kay later when she calmed down then kissed her cheek and walk out to the back where my room was. I wanted to know what was in my trunk bad but long as ma was home that was dead cuz ma Jackie ant play that drug dealing shit let alone having drugs in her house. I didn't' do that either but where would I go with my new future, and I don't even know what it is so I would just have to wait her out. I knew she would go to bingo for 7:00 which mean no later than 6:30 she gone be pulling out, so I'm just gone lay low until then. Matter fact I'm going pull the car around to the back and put it right by my window, so nobody won't even think I'm home.

I checked my watch it was 5:45 so I decided to text Kay hey ma just checking on you and Baby J hope yah good hit me up then I went fixed me some home cooked food. Ma put down some roast and cabbage with sweet cornbread. That bomb shit turned my radio on and played that Big Moe Purple Stuff DC just to relax my nerves a bit. Just like I thought 6:30 came and ma came asked me for 20 bucks to go with her play-ing money at bingo. Some shit about the 750 jackpot gone be hers tonight. She say that shit all the time and walk away a donator more than anything, but it keeps her happy, so I'm cool with it. I'm just glad she not on drugs and in them streets like most people she come up with. Anyways though she jumped in her lil Honda and hit the road. I knew she would be there until 8:30 or nine so that would give me plenty time to see what Big Red done dropped on me soon as she cleared the block

I went to the trunk nothing look out of place nigga must hire some professionals to do his work cuz from necked eyes shit look just as it should be, so I removed the floor rug and lifted up the spare tire. Man I damn near shit and pissed all at the same time from what I saw.

I came across five bricks of raw cocaine looking like lil yard bricks wrapped in tape. Guess that's why the first person started calling them bricks. Looked like maybe a five-pound bundle of grade A Hydro Cali bud one-thousand k-pack of x-pills and another 2 k-pack of Xanax bars all just sitting there with a envelope and a note. I picked up the envelope and the note to read the note. Look inside the envelope and soon all big face 100's look like about 2,500 or better. Man this nigga the truth done gave me a gold mine and some bread at the same damn time. Was all I thought for take moment. Then I read the note. It stated never play where you lay. Take this bread open you a spot no school zones no churches preferred a dead end. Shot gun house with few neighbors ant no pressure on no money so don't rush shit make ya move and take ya time when you done get at me I want 20 a brick on the raw. The rest is a gift. Get me my 100,000 K in a proper time then we gone talk again. Remember quiet money is the best money don't lose ya head, Big Unk.

Man I took a step back for a sec to refocus and put my plains in motion. This that change you life shit for real I thought to myself.

I took everything out my trunk and put it in my black

gym bag I'd wore to school and took it to my room. I knew I couldn't leave the shit in my mom house, so I tucked it in my closet behind the wall in a lil spot I had made since I was selling weed at school. I would leave it there until I figure out what I would do next and find me a spot to push out of.

You know I had to hit my man Zilla say what's good bro I asked nothing much just making rounds you know how that goes well nigga I'm gone pull up on you in 20 I said letting him know we needed to talk business so we hung up when we told each other where we would mete at our lil spot Will-D's Seafood on Highland Ave in our lil hood South Park.

I made it to Will-D's first in like 15 mins after our phone call Will-D be empty on the inside cuz everyone like to call their food in and just pick up instead of wine and dine so I chose to make Will-D's my meet spot to talk business with my closest people I would just pay Will-D's a hundred in advance so when I would come threw I would talk business and not be disturbed plus we would still order food a win win and good business. I went sat to the far back in my usual booth and waited for Zilla to pull up just like clockwork bro pulled up but to my surprise bro wasn't alone bro had guess who with him??? Yep, you guessed it Mrs. Candy was with my nigga that was cool and all but I don't talk business in front of Hoes so my attitude was a lil off and bro felt it. Damn nigga what's good he asked shit bro we got business to talk on and you bring company on top that to our meet spot man we don't know her like that I stated meaning every word. Then bro replied nigga you turned her on to me shit I thought she was cool my nigga meeting my frustration.

Excusing Candy by telling her to go sit and wait in the car me and bro went to our spot in the back of Will-D's. say bro my bad for spazzing a bit but nigga this shit real and that was a surprise seeing her like that. I mean yea she cool and all but I'm bout to put you up to some new shit and we got to be together with this one. This ant that same shit we been on this the big break we both need I stated while looking over the menu. Call Candy back in lets grab some food then we will get back to this money shit later back at ya spot on Euclid enough said. Zill replied and called Candy back in the restaurant to see if she wanted something to eat. Hey, Jay, she stated sitting down, what's good Candy, good to see ya again without the crew hugh I asked yea yo brother said he thought we should chill when I went to his car earlier that's right I stated just treat my brother good I stated then we all order to go plates as I apologized to Candy for snapping crazy thing she understood which let me know she was more hip than I thought so I put that in my memo box to watch her moves more closely. We left Will-D's and went our own ways not talking about shit that I had planned on but that was cool I needed more time anyways I pulled up to Pappa's Store in the hood off Haddox Street where most the homies hang and jumped out the lack to go grab a pack of blacks and a Big Red 20 oz soda and some Jolly Ranchers for my Texas Tea I would be going pick up when I left the store. When I stepped out the car I dapped up some of the homes I'd fuck with my nigga Co-Bo, Spoon, Coop, Mike G, and a few more but I couldn't help but notice while I was talking to lil Brice that Quinton kept looking at me all salty, but I didn't pay it no mind. I know how niggas be hatting on their own hood niggas, so I tried to shake it off. I know it's all about that time on Elgie when I beat him and the lil nigga duck out of 3,500 on the dice game niggas was talking that big money shit only had peanuts so I broke them nigga in front they bitch and talk cash shit so I know them nigga still sour but fuck that what's good Big Brice I asked dabbing my nigga up what its looking like out here on these South Park streets same old shit my nigga stated back say homie hit me later when you on chill I'm on my way to the big leagues and I got season tickets for you year round ya dig? Brice being the street nigga he is knew exactly what I meant but I don't think he knew how big I was talking them niggas new I get money but not on no big scale so I could see the nonbelief in cuz eyes when I spoke it to him, but I knew a nigga stomach wouldn't let him sleep on me cuz we done got money together before, so niggas know not to sleep on me. When I come back out the store, Quinton was still looking crazy so being me I trew a $20 bill at the nigga told him to keep the change then drove off laughing. The whole time these niggas clowns homie and that shit make my dick hard seeing a nigga hate.

Bout eleven pm I pulled up on Euclid at Zilla lil trap spot and backed up in the driveway I didn't like hanging at trap spots cuz that shit fifty-fifty laws come any time, so I just sat in my car with the lights off a.c. on music low and powed up me a four of my Texas Tea and put some on my black with the double dip for extra taste that's a street nigga heaven just ask any nigga from Beaumont to Houston shit go down. With that Pat playing in my ear Ghetto Dreams. I powed me up a cup when my candy's melted then texted Zilla cuz I'm outside at ya trap on Euclid. But he replied I be out in a sec cuz was in the kitchen wippen chickens when I pulled up. Zilla was fucking with them niggas on that north side for the sand some cats from P.V. Watts bread niggas but them boys prices was out the roof so I barley sent money they way anyhow cuz came outside and jumped in and reached straight for the cup fo I knew it I punched Zilla straight in his shit cuz beefed for me back then we just rocked the car for about three full minutes that's just how we was it was all love with us that's just how shit went hanging round us fight together eat together fo sho ride together brothers for life. After we cut the bullshit we got down to business I told cuz we need a new spot on a dead end with few neighbors we thought on it for a sec then remembered some houses for rent on Church Street where his ant sis stayed a cool part of the hood low key. That was the perfect spot so first thing in the morning we gone slide trew and pay the notes they asking I got some shit coming my way I told him and if we do it right we gone be good for good this go round you know bro was all in then the nigga hit my drank and killed the cup jumped out laughing and ran in the spo. Pay back a bitch homie know I'm gone down his shit tomorrow so I just powed up the rest and drove off. While I was on the move my phone rang I didn't' recall the number so I answered like I was sleep hoping it was Kay. Hello, a female voice said you sleep I'm sorry she kept talking while I was trying to pick up on the voice, so I said its cool who this? Oh this ya Sunshine she said all sexy I could tell she was smiling so I said what's good with you ma she said she was hungry and wasn't nothing to eat and could I bring her to grab some food from some where she also offered to pay gas and buy mines win win shit I'm on my way where are you I asked really not hungry or needing no gas I keep my bitch on F it's the only way to roll so you know that wasn't my real reason for agreeing I wanted to see what was real at 12:30 at night ant much open but legs at that time so she told me she was still at 1400 Brockman Ave Cardinal Sq #4. Jaz apt [my new spot]. I thought yea cool I'm gone text when I pull up I'm bout 5 minutes away so be ready I told her just so I wouldn't be waiting, or Jen wouldn't run out when I pulled up and blow the door off my plot when I pulled up I could see the light on dem in the front room but not much movement fuck around and might stay the night I thought. Then I texted Sunshine to let her know I was outside she was ready and out the door in no time you know I like that. Soon as she hopped in my phone rang it was my nigga Brice hitting me from earlier on what I told him. I told bro hit me soon as he open his eyes so we could take a ride and that was that I knew my G was gone be game with the rest.

Me and Sunshine drove off and I asked her where she wanted to get some food from she said it didn't matter Waffle House anything that was still open. Then she did some moe shit that trew me for a loop. She went in her purse and pull out all her money to hand to me. Here Jay was all I heard not knowing what was going on I just looked at her and asked what's that for I'm cool on gas she laughed this way more than gas money you want me to count it she asked I say shit why not. When she was done lil mama had like $4,500 cash on her so I asked where she worked she said she don't but she know how to get money so I said if I take this money you gone be broke for two months then she laughed and said if I take that money she would have more in 2 hours enough said so I took the money wasn't no need to ask no more question. Sunshine mind was made so was mine my new lil bitch and I was thinking with my dick head not to say I did get some head though too and from Waffle House.

When we pulled back up to Cardinal Sq. I decided to get out and see what was good when we walked through the door Jen was on the couch Jaz was in the kitchen and Candy was at the table playing on her phone soon as I walked in the moods switched everybody got happy it felt like. Hey Jay was all I heard then Jen said how you got with Jay Jessica? With a lil attitude so I lied, she ran into me at Waffle House when some nigga was giving her hell bout some shit, so I told the nigga to leave that Sunshine was my sister and that was the end of that. I don't know why I lied but I wanted to see how far all this shit would go and what would come from it crazy part they still had weed and liquor to drink from the night before.

We all took shots and started playing cards for shots while Candy look at me kind of crazy for a few times and I knew then from what I felt earlier back at Will 'Ds Candy was gone be one I would have to watch.

CHAPTER 7

Four Years Later:

Damn ma why you got to push shit to the limit all the times I can't change what's done I mean long story short you pushed me out ma and shit happened. None of it was planned I mean damn its hurting me to tell you this but the man in me want let me deny what mine.

Was the conversation me and Kay was having when she came back to me three years later Baby-J was five going on six and Jay Jr. was just turning 4. Kay had come back to me once I'd got my shit up and running life was cool then one day while at Jaz spot she broke down to me and told me her son was mine me and Jay Jr. was tight than a bitch cuz while Kay stayed gone I was around the whole time Jaz had Jay Jr. I didn't think much of it when she named him after me shit I was daddy too them all her spot was my spot, and everything went on over there we all fucked each other and became one big family so when she name him Jay Jr. she just said she want him to be just like me. Hold time she knew that was my boy so when she told me we went and got tested just to be sho and I'd be damn sho nuff shit stank lil man was mine. It didn't stop shit cuz I kept Jay Jr. with me all the time anyway. Candy and Zilla would fuck and shit from time to time but that never grew to nothing serious for on Zilla was married so we both ant trip when we told each other about the way she fuck that just the way it went but we never touch a nigga girl that's just law.

Jen still my lil bitch and gone fight fuck and buss a 50 fifty for a nigga she just can't wait till I say she my girl, but she know not to push that shit on me cuz that might get her cut off. Jaz spot still the spot for us all but they all done got there own lil places that's just how it had to be with all the shit that's moving I had to have different spots to hide my shit. Sunshine is a true bread winner lil mama been on a money train from day one and still on go her spot is the spot I'm at the most she just know all the right shit to say and do so I use her as an escape type. Kay came home twelve months back when I bought a new house for her and Baby-J my lil nigga had got big on me and it felt good to see them back at home feel like I finally got all I wanted after all that bull shit 22 and I got a peace of mind now I got to break this news to kay and start the drama all over again just last week the DNA test came back for Jaz baby boy and the lil nigga truly is mine good though cuz now we don't have to change no names the lil nigga earned it so to say but Kay not gone go for that shit a baby for another woman what the fuck was I thinking all I can do is tell her and hope she can understand cuz if not I know this the nail in the coffin right here. So I planned a nice dinner for just us two. At least just that way she won't space out and beat my ass in public when I break the news. Shit I went all in for this one. Cuz deep down I knew this would be the last meal.

When we arrived to the grill in downtown Beaumont they had a live band playing, candles on our table and a dozen roses laid out for Kay. Looking all good and everything set up right I got the worst response ever so I knew it was about to only go downhill form there. Nigga what's up no thank you are nothing just a bad vibe right off jump so I just let her talk nigga you better of not fucked none of my sisters matter fact they wouldn't stoop that low that almost pissed me off but I let her go on ya probably done fucked one of my cousins yea that what you did sorry ass, and on she went we ant even order food yet and I couldn't even be mad cuz for the first time she wasn't wrong but never would she guess what it really was so I just let her vent then I asked was she threw. We ordered and made the best out of the next few mins after she realized how beautiful things really was around us so I let her enjoy that then I ordered a glass of champaign to set the tone and I just went in., say bae I need to tell you something and I don't want you to flip out just try to understand before I could finish she was standing to leave so I grabbed her hand and just asked nicely for her just to listen then I started. I'm sorry I fucked up but I didn't cheat on you this time when I said that she looked puzzled and confused nigga what? I didn't' cheat on you when I did this so forgive me for that and look past it and move on ok nigga what you talking about she said so I just spilled it. I got a three-year-old son was all I could say fo she slapped me with tears on her face and pushed everything on the table on my lap before running out the restaurant. I just sat there for a sec picked up the candle and asked for the check with food all on me the Grill owner came over and asked was all ok and I replied probably never again with three hundred dollar bills in my hand to pay the bill and the tips when I made it outside Kay was getting in a taxi telling him to drive off. I walked in front of the car and held him up went to his window and gave him a 100-dollar bill and told him to bring her wherever she want to be safely and stepped back knowing that would probably be the last of Kay.

CHAPTER 8

Five years later and I still ant hear from Kay Baby-J would be 11 going on 12 and Jay Jr. 9 going on 10 my lil nigga to Jay Jr since I found out that was my son me and baby boy be together day in, and day out making moves and pick ups when he at school is the time I deliver the work to the spots when he out all we do is collect bread like clockwork. Big Red been making shit jump for me and my whole team. Boys don't like that shit either I took a small loss for a book that I had a Candy house but that ant stop shit just bussed one down and made two and get that right back some shit bout somebody broke in her shit while she was out and found the brick in her dish washer under the bottom where the motor housed at sound like bull shit to me but I keep my cool while the laws dusted for fingerprints. Besides that shit was on the up. Lil Brice had Washington Blvd. on lock and Church Street was zooming 24/9 no days off had a lil spot in Washington Manner that my nigga Sammy was running. Had a spot-on Gladys that Bottany ran on the North side shit everybody was eating I see how Big Red could make all that money and look like he don't move a muscle. He just keep good shit and good prices and pass shit out trew the city and pick up a big check all in one wrap. While the nigga at work the whole time. So how can the Feds hook you to anything when you at one place all the time being good boy. I was learning a lot from Big Red but I was in them streets that why our visits got shorter and shorter he refused to be seen with anybody working Zilla was on his best shit too Euclid was a new place shit brought that bag in plus the spot on Elgie and the one on Park man nigga couldn't keep them spots with enough shit each time I would drop off I would be on my way back good shit for the low always flew even cats from out of town was on a slide trew to grab and go sit was good just like planned.

Today was Saturday and on Saturdays we would all go meet up at Alice Keith Park and trow BBQ and fish fries and bet on the lil niggas B-Ball games same shit this day we all met up at A.K. park Zilla Brice Bottany, Sammy, Jason and me got that bitch crackin we bought food drinks music anything you needed the whole hood came out kids ladies you name it bmt was in A.K. Park so we cranked up a dice game and Quinton and Duck came to put they shot down to trying to roach up on some shit but who care money everywhere shoot a hundred bet a hundred the smallest thing. Shot was a twen-ty I hit on dice five pointes straight broke Quinton and Duck at the same time again them niggas was mad trying to go against the grain so I laughed at them fuck niggas we stayed at it in AK till the fuck boys come cleaned us out but some odd reason I felt somebody watching me as I got in my car to leave so when I pulled off I pulled off slow looking at everything around me and every car next to me so I could be show that I wasn't trippin if I saw the same head lights twice when I pulled off when I made it to the first light they had plenty cars behind me and on side me so shit was cool for now so I turned right to see who would all turn right. Some went straight but the forth car turned right to so I drove straight headed to the highway away from my spot just to see would the car come too. Just like I thought when I made it to the freeway the other car wasn't far behind, so I jumped on and took the next exit just to be sure bout five cars back the same car did the same shit, so I swung back around and headed back to the hood with a trick up my sleeve. I made it back to South Park and pulled up on Brandon at the lil homie J.Q. spot and parked on side the road then I hopped out and ducked on side my car with my 40 in my hand just like I expected the car pulled up tint-ed windows going slow so I jumped from behind my shit and ran up pistol drawn on the driver of the car and snatched the door open the bitch started screaming and shit when I put that iron to her head and asked what's good as I placed her car in park with my other hand.

Crazy shit ever it was Candy in a whole nother nigga car, so I look all around the car to see if someone else was in it before I went all in on the bitch and snatched her out the car shit wasn't addin up first my work a week ago now you following me look bitch talk I said full of fire as I pushed her to the passenger side and got in the driver seat. Bitch talk I said what you on my tail for hoe?

CHAPTER 9

What Candy told me fucked my head up had me looking at shit different but I just had to see I just had to put it all to the test so I started putting shit in motion bitch told me my own crew was plotting on me and my own brother had someone take the book, Duck and Quinton to be exact after she told me these things and what they were planning to do next and why they told her to follow me, cuz wherever I went they was to catch me coming out and off me whenever id move again. Then I thought back to all the shit that went on with Candy and new she would be the problem, so I drove to Hillebrand Road and told her she did a good job, and to text Zilla and tell them I'm at Jaz apt #4 just to see the reply before I made my mind to off her or let her live. Zilla passed the test cuz instead of letting her text I did it I just used her phone and turned mine all the way off so it wouldn't ping off no towers nearby I text Zilla while Candy ate my dick thinking that's all it would take for me to forget the real shit Zilla text came back 5 mins later asking what was she talking about that she must texted the wrong nigga man that shit made me smile. Hoe lied on my brother. But I can't say the same on the other two niggas, so I let her finish the job while I look for Quinton and Duck number. Bingo Duck I should have new a snake gone be a snake regardless, so I texted Duck phone Jay in Port Arthur on 17th and Charleston, the big house on the corner by himself and sent it right before I came. I stopped Candy didn't want my DNA on her body so I just held back and started wiping the steering wheel down and anything else I'd might have touched while I was on the driver's side while waiting on the text back. Show nuff the text came ok ma Conor House right car outside was the question so I just laughed and texted yea then deleted the text to him and Zilla. Then I told Candy good job that she was my girl and we gone go get my shit back form them clowns if she was down. Feeling good, she sat up and said lets ride daddy I said right after I piss baby hold up right quick while I step out I opened the door and when I stood straight up I said baby I'm gone hold you down to the end for this one then let off two shots to her head party over bitch I whipped the doors down and the phone and closed the car and jogged off to a yard I'd seen a bike in front of and jumped on it and rode back to J. Q. spot I trew the bike in my trunk and drove off headed to P.A. the back way when I got a few blocks up by a empty lot I grabbed the bike wiped it down and dumped that bitch I was on a mission and couldn't shit stop me I pulled up in P.A on 17th and Charleston twenty mins later. Parked on side the street and hid in the neighbor's yard behind the garage show nuff 15 mins later I saw a red car coming slow I knew the car cuz it was Duck bm car so I just laid low and watch as he went down the street to park where he could watch me come or go. Bingo I said when he parked behind a truck a few houses down I jumped the back fence and came up on Ducks car from the back walking cool calm like a regular person I knew he wouldn't expect nothing being out of town so late with nobody knowing he was there so I walked right to the car looking for alight with my hood on my head then I tapped his window may I please get a lite I said with a groggy voce like a dope feign would do so he leaned up and pushed the car light in and hit the dome light while he was doing that I was aiming my pistol trew the crack in the glass on the other side of my hoodie pocket nigga never saw what hit him pow 2 to the head now you know he dead as I jogged of the same way I came trew the back yards and over the fence back to my car. I took Savanna back to Beaumont turned down a back street by two bodies of water and emptied my gun I trew the bullets one way in the water and the gun the other way in the water wasn't' no need to have a hot bitch on me all the way back to Beaumont. I also avoided all stoplights and cameras that could place me anywhere near Port Arthur. When I made it back to BMT I turned my phone on and called my ma just to let my phone ping in South Park BMT TX at that same time boy what's wrong at 12 in the morning you calling me? Nothing ma just wanted to see if you was up cuz I be home soon and can't find my key I lied just so she would chill out.

CHAPTER 10

The next morning I woke up, I got dressed and checked my phone. I had two missed calls from Zilla, and a text read say bro hit me when you get up shit ant right. I thought to myself tell me about it I couldn't help but feel some type of way why would that Hoe say that about my right-hand nigga the other two yea but Zilla I got to look in to all this shit. I hit Big Red on the burn phone and set a appointment to get shit squared like it goes man when I touched that first 100,000 that shit wasn't nothing I was hitting for 36,000 a brick on the break down a thousand a zip the lowest I would go was 700 a zip bringing in 25,000 a brick so I would put up 12-18 thousand free money easy a day or a week I did three runs at 20K a brick then the rest was all me for 17K a brick cash up front now I'm charging cuts 22 a brick hold for 800 a zip breakdown my traps push for 850 or 900 a zip and that's what I use to pay my people. Money good just say I crawled then I ran in no time ya dig. I was going meet Big Red with a nice amount of bread just to keep shit 100 even thought I was a week before time he had a house I would bring the money too and that would be it he never met me there or nothing just drop and go then I would get a text to pick up a car from such and such and my shit would be there all the time never fail shit was tight so once I took care of shit with Red I hit Zilla say man meet me on Church ASAP bet was all said.

We made it to Church Street bout 3:30 and shit felt strange so I watched Zilla every move when he got in the car we dabbed up like normal then he broke the ice say nigga what's up with Candy he asked I said what you mean say bro she sent me a crazy text last night about you at Jaz house and shit you think she trying to set you up and texted the wrong phone cuz I texted back and she ant hit yet shit just was crazy nigga what you think of it he asked Shitea, I don't know what to make of it hit her and see what she say while I'm with you and we can go from there. My nigga ant waste no time to call on speaker but the phone went straight to voice mail like I knew it would. Then I said something crazy going on cuz believe it or not she told me you sent people in her spot to grab that brick I had there, nigga what Zilla said looking lost nigga what the fuck I'm gone shoot for one brick when we play with 10 or better at a time nigga fuck shit she on Homie? Same shit I said my nigga cuz she up to something we might have to take her out Zilla stated I just looked like in deep thought then my phone went off it was Jaz calling so I thought about JR and answered what's good ma? Hey daddy she stated where are you? on the move I stated what it do ma? Man shit bad they found Resha dead about a hour ago on a road called Hildebrandt in her well in a car it wasn't her car and she was on the passenger side so whoever it was had to been driving and jumped out the cops think he from round them parts or had someone followed him or whoever it was I just looked at Zilla and shook my head say ma where my lil man I asked? He right here looking for you to come get him. Bet I'll be trew when I'm done let me know what the word is man. Ok daddy then see you later came next. Damn shit crazy I said to Zilla guess somebody else had it out for Candy more than us right. Zilla laughed and said cold world damn that was some good pussy gone to waste? Cuz you say some crazy shit I said then got back focused – nigga hit for that brick I'm trying to hit for that life – green mean go Zilla stated and looked me in my eyes loyalty before betrayal a motto we stood by and a reminder not to never switch over.

CHAPTER 11

I pulled up to Jen lil spot and got loose for a second and grabbed a different outfit to put on. I slide trew Jen spot from time to time just to keep s hit good. I keep clothes at her shit just to make her fill like her man gone come home any night and a reminder to keep niggas out my shit when I'm gone to long you know I'm daddy!

Then I slid trew Sunshine spot counted some bread and put hers and mine in the safe I got in her closet floor. Sunshine my girl man lil mama the real deal she go live and go get it if I didn't know her ways she would be the one, but we one in the same I guess that's why we so tight I beat that pussy good just because and washed off then burned out to my lil nigga Jay Jr when I got to 1400 Cardinal Sq #4 my boy was out the door soon as I pulled up when I stepped out the car lil man punched my leg where you been nigga? He said man who you talking to I ask him nobody he replied nigga ten think he run me and shit I picked him up and bit my nigga neck while his mama stood and watched in lust looking good than a bitch like always might have to put lil Jay to sleep and rock mama world then my phone rang. Bitch ass nigga I'm gone show you! a pussy nigga screamed then hung up in my face I caught the voice tho it was that pussy Quinton so that nigga just signed his death wish. I didn't even get mad cuz any nigga who tell you what they gone do ant gone do shit life taught me that, so I just played with Jr and beat his ass in Call of Duty and ate that shit Jaz cooked some chicken cheese noodle shit with shrimps in it with garlic bread shit was fire no lie. Me and baby boy stayed at it till like 1:00 am. When I got with Jr all problems go out the door. My lil nigga fell asleep on the couch and I got horny instantly. So I walked up on Jaz and bit her ass check she jumped, and I grabbed her, pushed her to the wall and kissed her from ear-to-ear Jaz was a real lil bitch never complained stayed calm and on her shit I just couldn't make her my girl and fuck up all I had with everyone else, so I slid back more than forward, but best believe I beat that pussy like no other I ant even lying. Tonight was no different I beat the walls down made sure the neighbors new my name, then I got up to go to the store to get some blackes, candy, and Big Blue so I could do my thang while I watched Paid in Full and got head for the rest of the night. Texas Tea it is here I come addicted to drank and I love it.

On my way out the door shit felt funny like it just was in the air my senses locked in, so I turned and called Jaz say ma grab the .45 and watch the door while I get in my car when I drive off lock up and put Jr in the bed. I told her she did just as told as I got to my car I could just fill it, so I took my 9mm and put it on my lap then burned off looking in my mirror the whole time.

I pulled up at the Florida store and looked at the time it was 1:50 am that was late but not for a street nigga so I had to be careful the cops be looking for young black niggas out at that time of night so I grabbed my shit and made it back to the car I just couldn't shake that filling so I fired up a black plain something I never do just to set me straight no drank no nothing on my shit, shit taste a whole lot different to I put the Lac in reverse and backed out then drove off no car was on the road but mine but I could still feel someone watching me in my head so I drove slow just looking up down all around I rode by my mom's shit just to check then I passed by Jen shit just to check really looking for a tail so I didn't stop nowhere just rode slow and looking then I made it back to 1400 Brockman and the filling hit me harder like something was right there waiting or just watching me. So I just sat in the car not wanting to bring harm to my son way so I called Jaz and told her to grab the .45 and watch the peephole I could tell this time I made her worry but it was real I felt it so I looked all around trew my dark tent, cocked my shit, grabbed my stuff then opened my door soon as the door opened the wind hit me even that shit was strange knowing something was wrong I walked slow to the door just like I thought three niggas jumped out on me and pushed upon me I started to blast off then I thought of being out numbered and my son that's right behind them walls all I was hoping was Jaz didn't open the door but lil did I know that what exactly she was gone do all I heard was boom from the .45 I dropped all my shit one nigga ran and the other two started poppin all I could think was don't let them in the apt so against all odds.

I let my 9mm bang not too much for me but to keep them from the Apt. so I took it all boom I bussed pow pow they bussed boom, I let off moving towards the back of my car away from the Apt. in plain sight, boom I hit one cuz he dropped his shit but that was short lived cuz the one that ran caught me on the blind side and hit me two to the back I went down but kept buckin until my shit clicked I saw them nigga run away and help the one I hit that made me proud I kept them niggas away from Jr was all I could think as I blacked out and heard Jaz screams and cries stay up please help please help as the neighbor Mrs. Q came from upstairs to help the situation then it all went blank.

Chapter 12

Five years a long time to be laid up in a coma I woke up July 31, 2017, Baby-Jay was 17 going on 18 and Jay Jr was turning 16 in a month. My boys had done grew up and thanks to all the clothes and shoes and money I sent to Kays mother Baby Jay still had mad love for his daddy lil did I know Baby-J wasn't Baby-J no more and J-Jr wasn't lil Jay Jr no more either them lil niggas was young savages to the heart lil did I know Baby-Jay and Jay-Jr was paying more attention to everything I was showing and teaching than I knew. Everybody wanted to pull the plug said I was suffering. My sisters Shanae and my sister Mesha they both gave up on me, but Ma Jackie wasn't having none of that all she would say was God ant gone let that happen so for five long years mama Jay came to the nursing home I was staying at to sit with me and quote scrips from the god Book, even brought my boys on weekends so that way they could never forget me. When I came back to it I couldn't remember shit not even my name at first I was lost. The night I got hit up the bullets had hit a main vein so I had to be rushed to surgery so they could stitch it back together before I bled to death. While in surgery I slipped away twice and the last time I stayed sleep I fell into a coma where I been the whole time in a deep deep sleep. Once my mom told me what went down I started to remember that night like yesterday. Three niggas I recall mask on and hungry. Then I thought about Jay Jr, so I ask for Jay Jr right away. Ma said he good and that was him by my bedside when I woke. That grown lil man was Jay Jr. all I could see was that lil boy I'd beat on the game all night long, so I asked how long was I under It's been five years today ma said. I was at a loss, so I just laid back and asked to see my boys. In came two big boys but I could see all in their face that that was my baby boys all grown up you could say I dropped a tear out my left eye for all the years I missed then I took a deep breath and smelled both of their heads I needed that to know from that moment on everything had just become real. My boys looked just like me all over again, so I asked Baby Jay how Kay was he said married and I was cool with that just happy she let Baby Jay be by my side when I needed him most. I look to Jay Jr and saw the pain in his eyes I knew it was a lot I would hear about when I got my shit together, so I just smiled to the thoughts in my head.

It took me four months to get all my shit back right

my walk, my talk, my strength, my words was off all type of shit body had sores from being in bed so long I had to shake back head all big body all small man I ant even know me no more.

I went stayed back with my mama so I could rest and work out I took vitamins and creatine to build my muscles back up. I ate just to eat so I could blow back up in two months at moms house. I was just about back to 100% in my head and in the mirror. Jen would come by and eat me up, Jaz showed up and washed my ass, Sunshine keep my money right even for the whole five I was out. I had took some losses but not with Big Red or nobody so that was still good cuz I started paying up front and making 100% profit, but some niggas ran off some spots got shut down some went to jail and Zilla was still at it looking out for moms the whole time so every doubt I had about my brother was out the door. Bro was still on his shit but not like we was his plug was no Big Red so shit wasn't as sweet but it made do I went to my closet and moved the wall I had been made way back in school just to check and it all was still there, no drugs I been moved that shit never play where you lay but that money that took its place was still there with my chrome 50 piece and my two .45s that I'd never used so the first thing I did was counted 20,000 and went put it in ma's draw for all she been trew with me I still had ten to play with so I called my boys. Baby Jay was driving and doing his own thing now getting ready to finish school. When he pulled up he had Jay Jr with him, them niggas became close than a bitch crazy part Jay Jr went found Baby Jay when Jaz told him about his brother who was also a part of P.A. Texas like Jaz was so with a lil help and Facebook them nigga hooked up and been down ten toes ever since. See Jay Jr young but the nigga move like a O.G. in the game and don't take not shit from no one? My boys pulled up and came in the house Baby Jay had a jeep he got from his ma for being on his shit so that's what they pulled up in what's up I stated to my Little Me's. what's good pops? Shit ya'll are I replied I called for a favor I said looking serious at them both what's up pops they both said, man I'm down right now and I need some change to get me by. I thought I was gone hear some shit like daddy we broke, or we got a few bucks type shit but that ant what I heard them lil niggas both went in they pockets and started counting bread real bread they both pulled of like five large and handed it to me like is that cool? I just was lookin dumb like what the fuck did I miss all this time. Then Jay Jr spoke say pops don't be mad, but I checked ya spots we would pull up and told lies to ya workers that I was to pick up what was owed I would get Sunshine to bring me by to drop the spill cuz I knew she would ride if a nigga bucked me then I went to Jen and told her she know where the work comes from, and we need to eat. Jen did know some niggas who was plugged but I wondered how Jay Jr new that I ant never use none of Jens people to get up in the game, but I guess she made it happen for Jay Jr.

Then he said he hit up Zilla and told Zill to hold him down that I had told him to do these things if anything ever happened remember Jay Jr was only ten when all this happened I didn't know that lil nigga was taking that shit serious then he said he found his big brother and broke shit down to him but lil did he know Baby Jay had shit jumping back in P.A. at his grandma house when he came from school Baby Jay would move pounds of Dro at 2,500 a pound he was a school boy by day and a brick man till 10:30 at fourteen years ole so I guess them lil niggas was made for that shit well now that I know the truth I replied then ant no need to play with ya'll we gone keep the same shit going only we gone run this shit with family only cuz I don't know who to trust every since the nigga hit me. Yea pops Baby Jay said we even know that part too we got all ends on lock two of them niggas gone but one still stands we gone leave that one to you.

CHAPTER 13

Loyalty Before Betrayal

Riding in the back seat with my boys way damn cool. Them niggas had they own style and shit listening to a Kevin Gates nigga spit some hot hit I rode in the back with them niggas for the last past three weeks I wanted to check they moves them boys went to school by day total good boys straight goons by four o'clock I would get picked up like clockwork and just sit back I made them boy respect the rules no drugs in the car no smoking weed on the job and that's how we rode strapped up belts on playing by the rules. Them boys would pick up make drops and move just like bosses when someone wanted to grab they would meet at the trap house, wheel and deal and be out no games no hanging around just like daddy preached. Then my boys took me by a graveyard off Magnolia Street in the North end we got to see if you know these niggas. So we got down and walk to the grave site and on the head stones read Rest In Peace Quinton and his brother Juice I said yea I know them niggas what's good? Fuck nigga Quinton use to feel a way about me right before all this shit happened I said yea we know Baby Jay stated word on the streets was that's the nigga who came your way that night. Then Jay Jr spoke up yea heard ma and Sunshine and Jen all talking one day and they was talking about that night and what the streets was saying then ma said one day Quinton said some shit that gave him up he said damn ma trying to halla you a stand-up type chick even bus for your nigga he slipped and said and the only way a nigga would know that they had to be there so when I heard that Jay Jr said he knew that nigga had to die so I played the kid role and rode my bike around them niggas every day, but guess who them niggas stared hanging with pops Baby Jay said looking red hot so I asked who son and his answer almost knocked me off my feet nigga with yo fuckin brother Baby Jay said then looked me in my eyes.

Blood is blood no matter how it spills so I asked my boys ya'll think ya'll uncle set all that shit up? We not going by what we think pops we going off the way shit look I know all ya'll from the same hood but why would your brother hang with your enemies? That was a good question a 15-year-old and a 17-year-old was dropping jewels on me so I must be slippin, so I asked how ya'll caught these two niggas? Jay Jr spoke up see pops we look like lil kids niggas don't fear us which is the first mistake see pops I played on them niggas I rode my bike by every day stopped asked for dollars and let them nigga get loose then I started cleaning they yard and feeding their dogs so they dogs would trust me then one night I'd come by with Baby Jay in the back drop and knocked and call them niggas outside asking for money to go to the skating rink they started making fun of me and playing games say go ask my daddy and shit like that but I just was making sure it was just them two home when we saw it was Baby Jay walked up like he was waiting on me and them nigga ant even see what came next Baby Jay popped Quinton in the foehead and I hit Juice in the face then we took off running to the dope rental we had on the next street then drove off like it wasn't shit. Man that was a cold hit from some young g's I had to give it to my lil niggas them boys wasn't no game, so the next shot was all on me.

CHAPTER 14

Next morning on a Saturday I had Baby Jay bring me to the car lot so I could cash out something live it was time to get back to the mix shit would get fixed and things was going to start happening, so I need to get my bread up not for me but for my whole family. I bought a gray 745 Light tint no rims just wanted to look bossy that's all no glitter no glam. When I left the car lot and got my insurance squared up I went met up with my girl. Sunshine see Sunshine stayed g' the whole way I knew it was something about her from day one now I know she the one. I went to my safe in the floor in her closet and opened it up last I checked it was at 30g's but boo been adding on for a nigga so I had to count the gains I was up to 50 that was a good look Sunshine damn near matched my pockets while I was on my back, if that ant a good bitch what do you call it I grabbed the bread and strapped it to me like it go then called Sunshine in the room. Say girl come here I told her she ran to me looking confused and all so I played the part bitch close the door I yelled she shook then pushed the door closed then I pulled her in the closet where the fuck is my money bitch I stated just to see her jump she look in the open safe at it being empty then she grabbed her mouth and said I don't know daddy did you move it so I went in deeper oh now I'm a damn fool it's all my fault now my shit gone so I moved it that's it right? What about that nigga you let know the code to my shit and he made off with my bread what about that part I said with a straight face she stared to cry and said I don't bring niggas over that's why it's your clothes in the closet and your money no one else so I turned the gas u bitch strip down ass necked and said firm and mean. She froze for a bit, so I screamed now bitch right the fuck now she grabbed her shirt over her head exposing her bra, then unhooked her pants I screamed again hurry the fuck up she damn near fell trying to get the pants off her legs take that Hoe ass bra off and them draws whole time I'm in lust like a bitch! looking at this sexy smooth skin. Bitch get necked pussy showed and titty on salute this gone be the first pussy I had in five hold years I thought to myself still with a straight face put ya fuckin head in the safe I said until you see my money, crying and all she bent down hands and knees to put her head in the safe don't come up till you see my money bitch since I'm crazy all of a sudden. So while she was down head in the safe I stroked my piece till it rocked up then I dropped down on one knee behind her I said don't lift your head till you see my money bitch. I mean that shit. I yelled at her just to shake her up then I ran my shit in her dry and hard just to fuck her nerves up she buckled for a sec then shot straight back up I spit on my shit to get it wet then I went in soft she didn't deserve no ruff shit so wasn't no need to go overboard so I slow stroked until I felt that pussy get greasy I squeezed them ass cheeks then rose up in it loving every min. of the shit. I went slow then fast then slow then deep then short strokes then up and out then down and to the side I was just playing in her shit cuz this what she earned whole time her head still in the safe hitting shit same time shit was funny to me just to see how acting mad make a person do the most crazy shit that's why I say fear is better than love I know I play too much but role play make shit last, so I was just role playing and enjoying my powers. Then to play even more I asked do you see my money yet she said no daddy I'll make it all back for you just let me work so I went deeper and faster till I was close to nutting then I pulled out a stack and started spanking her with money then I asked how you gone make 50 g's with ya mouth or ya ass cuz cant nobody touch my pussy I said leaning in to go all the way fast as I could then I started letting money fall by the safe door while I asked do you see my money yet bitch? She said yes so I said well move ya head and get my shit then I nutted all on side her face just when she pulled her head out the safe I rubbed it on her lips and said I'm gone call CPS for child endangerment you keep biting on kids we laughed she got up then kissed my shit and said now who in control with my dick in her mouth I just stood there cuz deep down she knew better than to bite my shit so I just put them eyes on her while she sucked me back hard when I got there I fucked her right there on shoes and all regular style eye to eye fuck it I'm gone make her fall in love she earned it five years and some change even rode for my lil nigga shit a boss bitch indeed the game was good to me so I was going to be good to the game just with some whole new players and a whole new vision let the game begin clutch time player.

CHAPTER 15

I went home and got me some well needed rest from all the shit I'd heard and learned over the past few weeks from my lil Hittas I knew that life as I knew it would never be the same.

From all the shit with Quinton to Juice, even that fuck nigga Duck who was found in his baby's mother car dead in Port Arthur two day after I'd got shot word in the streets nigga was in P.A creapin and got hit up by some bitch man who pulled up on him. Was the word on that issue. Then I thought long and hard on my own brother Zilla. See me and Zilla not only real good patinas but we found out years back we both had the same pops but growing up in different homes gave us different ways but since we hooked up we been down like four flats from Jump Street. So shit be kind of hard to except when someone say shit about my bro cuz I think back to all the shit we did we snatched bodies together we rode together and the break down was always 50/50 so I couldn't bring my head around bro being responsible for my life misfortunes and sudden rains of bad luck, but the more I thought on it all the more shit added up and pointed more and more bro way. Let's think back on this all first it started when I told him bout the new work and plug I met. Nigga acted a lil salty when I'd never tell no names nothing too big on it though. Then he was the closes thing to Candy at that time cuz I'm the one hooked them up. I saw lil shit with that situation too but downplayed it cuz it always been bro's before hoes but one night when I'd popped up at Candy spot bro was there I had used my key and made myself welcome I had a book of raw on me for my lil niggas who moved shit around them parts. Boys had hit me up and said they would be ready by the next morning to rescore. Me not the one to ride with drugs I keep safe houses all around the city that I load up with just what I need for the people I set plays up with so when we meet up its nothing more nothing less case a nigga wanna try something funny like catching me with my reup or coming short. So I play on my own rules even when I'm on their field cuz when they come its grab and go no getting out the car no going in I jump in with them count the bread then jump in my shit and burn off when I'm clear I have my young niggas step out and bring the product strapped and ready so the money and the drugs never in the same spot. Anyways when I'd come in Candy's front door shit was quiet as normal so no need to interrupt I'd went straight to the kitchen and broke down the dishwasher like normal and placed the brick. You and I both know who gone think dishwasher if one ever did break in so that was the spot each time until it was time to be sold. As I put all the shit back like it goes the room door came open and Candy and zilla stepped out on some regular shit. Hey jay Candy said sup ma I replied but I couldn't help but see the look on Zilla face while he watched the dishwasher not one to speak my hand and knowing I caught his look Zilla asked that bitch still broke bro just to make light of it. I guess I replied as broke as it can get then we laughed, and all left the kitchen we talked shit for the next 30 mins or so then I got out there way and back on my mission. The lil niggas that the brick was for Ant hit the next day ready to score but to tell me that it's good and first thing in the a.m. they would grab that shit had been slow for them the rest of that night before, so I understood, and ant see no need to go move the work cuz in less than 24 hours them young niggas be to get it. Then I got a call the same night at about 10:30 saying someone broke in Candy's house I didn't keep money there or no shit, so I didn't really sweat it I just told her hit me when the cops left I didn't have no need to think Zilla cuz he was riding with me when we got the call. When the cops cleared out we pulled up I'd asked what was missing I could see the TV's gone look like some Jewels, and some small shit games spare phones like that shit lil niggas hit for when they break in. Just to go make a few buck then I made it to the kitchen me and Zilla and the dishwasher I could tell had been fucked with so I snatched the face off the bottom and the brick said look for me. Right then I thought Candy so I played cool and told Zilla one down, he asked what? looking confused then I aimed my two fingers at Candy back of her head like a gun explaining what I meant with no words said when Candy turned around I'd asked about my brick and all the questions you could think of she played that shit off so good fooled me how sneaky she was. Zilla just said cold like and we went got back in the car. First think Zilla asked was do I think she went out like that and all I could say was cold world. Then it was this shit with Quinton and Juice that fucked me up the most why would you start having these niggas around while I was in a coma all the way until that couldn't nobody tell me shit not Candy not the missing brick shit not even my own mamma when it came to Zilla and loyalty. But this part of the puzzle was too much I just couldn't place it I'd told my nigga about them niggas millions of times and one day I would off them niggas so what makes ya'll friends all of a sudden? All I know is I saw shit different from the day I left Magnolia Cemetery with Jay Jr and Baby Jay no nigga was to be trusted not even my own brother.

Fool me once shame on me! I made that clear in my head to never let doubt get the best of me for long as I live shit almost cost me my life and for that I was holding a king-sized grudge. Leaving Magnolia Street

I'd seen my nigga Jason from the North side of town. Me and Jason grew up real tight as kids then he moved to the North, but we kept in contact he ran the North while I did me in South Park. So when I saw my boy I had Baby-J pull up on him so we could chop game on things that had been going down even though Jason be on that North he knows what be going on in the South so I just wanted to hear the talk on the other side of town on thing in the streets. What's up Jason I yelled from the back seat my nigga was washing his Lack at the carwash just up the street on Lucas and Magnolia. Nigga Jay that's you he replied yea man! Man gets out and come fuck with me he said as I got out the back seat. We dabbed up and got straight to it nigga you gone let them niggas take you out huge he stated referring to my situation 5 years ago. Hell no nigga that's too hard I don't go that easy I stated. Then we laughed man come sit in the car he told me I got shit to tell you on all that he stated. So we jumped in his Lac while some base head washed the rims and shit. Then he got to it. What's up with ya brother Zilla nigga? He asked out the blue I stated he cool what's good man keep ya eyes on Zilla bro he be out here in Mada with this lil broad, and Homie do his thang on this end too word on the street nigga trying to take over South Park and branch out North so he been trying to hire help to get niggas wiped out down ya way and I can tell it gone all be some trow away shit cuz all the niggas he getting at is no names niggas trying to make a name long story short all flunkies. Jason dropped game to me and I just listened cuz Zilla ant told me shit about all the new shit that he had goin on I went in to a daze thinking it all out in my head then I heard Jason again nigga who he gone go to war with ant that many niggas still in the mix in ya hood like that last I knew ya'll niggas had shit just like it need to be Jason said then he named some niggas who was still at it in South Park, Big Fats, Stank, Lil C, just to name a few then he said but them niggas ant no threat then niggas all low key money and they all ready in line with ya'll so that only leave you and that Big Red nigga and can't many touch Big Red we even know on the North side that's a whole nother ball game. So what you think it's all for Jay, Jason asked, I couldn't say shit just told cuz good looking gave dap and told bro I'd hit him up more sooner than later.

I jumped back in the jeep with my boy and broke shit down too then like it had just come to me but then niggas had caught wind of some shit like that a few months back on their own. So what I did next was a no brainer. I called Zilla – sup from what's cracking I stated same shit lil bro what the word he asked making moves I replied trying to catch up with ya when ya time get right – but give me a honk he stated then we hung up.

Pops what's the deal Baby Jay asked ant shit going have a sit down with Big Unk Zilla you know how that shit goes.

Since its war let it be war I thought and got dropped off to my 745. When I got to my spot I'd gave Jay Jr the 50k I'd grabbed from Sunshine and told him the house to go drop to that I used to pay Big Red I told him to let them know that's from ya old man I would do the rest I told him. Then I hit Big Red – sup nephew Red stated when he picked up I just said a sit down and that's all needed to be said. Twenty minutes flat we was at the underground. This spot we'd only used for sit downs it's called the underground cuz all business is handled underground in a soundproof room that makes shit hard to pick up in case the feds had taps or anything underground was a drop zone dead no signal of any kind so that's where we talk real real real street shit.

CHAPTER 16

At the underground I explained to Red all that I was put up on Red knowing me my whole life new to take me serious so we made plans to destroy the enemy.

We talked numbers we talked guns we talked death cuz for sure someone was gone die and we had to put some insurance on my life cuz I wasn't gone stop at nothing and Red had people who have people so in no time my army count was trew the roof in no time and real niggas not trow aways. When that was done we went our separate ways with new niggas following me real close by but not too close to be seen hitters on deck is what you call that it was niggas by each one of my spots niggas by my mamma house niggas around everything that I valued that's how deep Red was and I new it just never wanted to see it. The hour past and I hit Zilla what's good fam I stated you he replied meet me at the studio in ten I replied bet and that's how that went.

We pulled up and went in the studio I didn't want to expose my hand so I played the come-up part instead of the violent part, say nigga I been down at the park for a lil min but I know some cats that can still put us where we need to be the same cats as before just with even better prices. Oh yea Zilla said matter fact who is those niggas you never once told me that so how can I keep trusting all that and know for sure we breaking everything 50/50 nigga you could be holding out on me nigga we been at this shit for years and look like you the only one moving up! So why my shit so short Zilla said a lil too ruff for my taste, so I played it cool and asked. Nigga what you stating?

The nigga snapped nigga I'm saying fuck your people I got my own shit going on. When you went down for 5 years you ant leave me no plug nigga I had to make moves to keep us both on float while you laid on your back playing sleep and shit! Nigga come to think about it you ant never tried to show me who to grab from incase shit went wrong like it did. Nigga all those year I know you was putting money up and not packing fare Zill went on and on like he felt that way for far too long. Truth be told I'd never held back when it came to the bread everything was 50/50 from the start to the end niggas just wanna see what they wanna see cuz even though we made the same we didn't live the same I invested and bought things that would last. Zilla went to the casino and took trips just because so that's

why shit ant look even. Then it all made sense this nigga tried to get me killed this nigga was double crossing
me from the start this nigga wanted me gone my own
brother I thought. So I looked up and that's when I saw
it the Devil all in one while the nigga said welcome back
brother take care of ya self as he stood to leave I'll see
you soon he said and turned his back to leave. I wanted
to squeeze right then and kill the whole problem, but
it would have all been a loss I would of for sure went
spent no less than 20 to life in a can if I would pull a
trigger just like that at my own spot on camera and the
last person for him to be seen with so I had to hold
back knowing shit was all over now!

CHAPTER 17

I left the studio and headed to Jaz spot I'd told her to grab as few items and just come on and leave the rest. I put Jaz up in the house I'd bought for Kay back in the day it never would get used cuz all I would do was cut the grass clean and push on I didn't want her in Cardinal Square knowing how shit was going to be. As for everyone else I left them where they was I just wanted to protect Jay Jr mom in case anything happen to me my boys would still have a mama. Then I ordered a hit on Euclid Trapp House and the one on Elgie at the same time they was cleaning that shit out I was at Zilla spot in Mada you want war, so I'm gone bring war see Zilla ant know I new about Mada we never talked on it or I'd never been there with him before. But Jason showed me the ends and outs of the spot, so I hit that bitch while my boys hit the rest. On Mada Zila wasn't there so I took all hit shit even his baby mama. When this war over wont nothing be standing except the last man never cross a brother!

Shut you bitch ass up hoe I stated to Zilla baby momma Shika when she woke up tied with her hands to her feet on her stomach laying on the floor in a bando house that was run down in the Pear Archer Area yea bitch ya'll all gone pay for ya snake ass baby daddy crossing me then I knocked the bitch back out it was on to the next the same night I had Baby Jay hit Zilla mama spot and snatch her up and bring her to the Bando in the Archer too.

Then we hit the nigga sister shit and snatched her up. We hit all that shit in a two-hour time frame both the niggas trap his main spot his mom and his sister now I was waiting o the nigga phone call cuz lil did he know I knew everywhere he was since he left the studio I had a car on the nigga tail the whole while. The nigga was on the North side with E-body and K-dug some made niggas from that way, so I put two and two together that's the nigga new plug so that's what turned it all sour the nigga feel he don't need a nigga no more sorry to tell the nigga them niggas ant close to Big Red fuck all that though cuz them niggas gone die to. I told the tail to keep a eye on them till I get there I was bringing smoke and I stood on that shit. I made it to the North off Helbing Road in bout 35 mins and pulled up to the house where them niggas kicked it at and waited until them niggas came out I brought four niggas with me, who stayed on go. Soon as them niggas came out we took over. We jumped the gate to gain access to the yard and just duck down on the dark side of the house soon as they step out all three of them we hit them up all leg shots cuz we was taking them niggas with us, back to the Pear Archer to meet his family.

CHAPTER 18

We had to move fast due to the gun shots we stripped them of they guns and placed them niggas in the back of the unmarked van while the lookouts I had tail Zila made sure shit was all good.

We had blood everywhere, but we made it. Hit two niggas in the knees and Zilla in the stomach fuck it I thought as we push off to the Pear Archard Bando.

Back at the Bando we had Zilla mom, his baby mama, his sister now him E-body and K-dug all laid on the floor tied, and duct taped so I slapped Zilla to get the nigga to focus and pay attention then I sat the nigga up with tape on his mouth and started talking to the nigga.

Blood is blood no matter how it spills I stated to the nigga then I told the nigga you turned on ya own brother for some fame and a name as I slapped the nigga the nigga just look like he would kill on the first chance, but I expected that cuz bro was far from Hoe in many ways.

Nigga just forgot the code Loyalty Before Betrayal and its going to cost his whole family even me I knew but death is the only answer to betrayal. I scooped his mother up so she could sit up against the wall across from Zill cuz I knew any nigga who could see his mom in harm way and cant do nothing for her would break any nigga so I moved her tape off her mouth and asked is it anything you wanna tell ya boy for the choices he has made she just look at me and said I loved you like a son shit shot chills trew my body cuz even though she wasn't my mom it was just like she was and after tonight shit would never be the same. I put the tape back over her mouth and feeling rage cuz the words hit so deep I shot his baby mama point blank in the back of the head just to hit somebody that would hurt but not as much as mom.

Zilla spazzed out at the sight of the shit but lil did I know Zilla had shit going on two at the same damn time cuz right then my phone rang. When I'd answered all I heard was son please no.

My mother fuckin mom yelled in my ear crying help me then smack somebody slapped her and took the phone. My blood shot trew my hoodie what the fuck I thought as I listened how them niggas get my mom while niggas was on guard? I'm gone kill Red was all I thought as I looked at Zilla who just sat there mad than a bitch.

Then the voice on the phone said yea bitch nigga a eye for a eye. War time pussy he stated while I tried to catch the voice then it hit me the nigga Brice snatched my mom! It's up Zilla had turned my nigga on me, and I didn't' even see it happening. Damn shit changed since I'd been out for them 5 years. Nigga you fuck up the money I'm gone fuck up ya life Bryce stated then made a request bitch nigga we need 20 bricks and 200,00k right now or fuck ya mama have shit ready in 40 mins or this bitch dead nigga when I hit back it better be all there and if you got Zilla with you tell him fuck him too you niggas dumb than a bitch let the money come between ya'll and maybe even pussy. I played you niggas the whole time. Bryce stated. Then hung up after saying see you in 40 bitch!

CHAPTER 19

Zilla heard the whole phone convo with me and Bryce and shit looked bad cuz it all made sense. Every since I had told Bryce to hit me to get that money with me the nigga played the game like a true playa from this missing brick at Candy spot to Duck and Quintin to the all-out war that was taking place right as we spoke. Bryce had the upper hand the whole time cool with both us and trusted by the whole team. Fuck I yelled out loud. Then dialed Jay Jr and asked him if he'd made good with the 50K I'd gave him he stated all good so I new that the bricks would be there that would be the easy part but all in all I only had sixty grand swinging to my name in all that wasn't close to what Bryce was asking 140K shy to be exact. Shit was adding up and problems I was knee deep in. I had a dead bitch that was like family on the floor my brother and his mom and lil sister taped up. Two well known brick niggas shot and taped up so that meant problems with the North Side too shit went all bad in one phone call and a nigga had the woman that meant the most to me my mother fucking momma!

Chapter 20

Zilla had told Bryce about the new moves he was making and the new plugs he had. He told Bryce me and him was never gone be the same from talks we would have Zilla felt us breaking apart and schooled Bryce for when the time came so Bryce would go with the new money team that Zilla was putting together. But Bryce wanted it all for self and made his own plans from the word go and the nigga played it to the T cuz now shit was way to deep to just overlook. So Bryce new the right time to strike when me and Zilla would wanna kill each other regardless and make off with a good name and all the drugs and kill us off all at the same time. I had to give props where props due the nigga snaked us and fucked the game up while doing it. So I just look at Zilla taped and shot then grabbed some old cloths and shit I could find and taped the shit to the nigga stomach to catch some the blood from where I shot him. Wasn't no need to talk lines had been crossed and shit was trew the roof so I walked over to his ma and kissed her as she moved her cheek from my lips and I said I love you like a mother hope you can ever understand then I just turned to leave the Bando knowing I wouldn't kill my brother or his mom in cold blood fo no true reason so before I left I hit K-Dug a E once in the head no need to leave them around knowing they would come for me anyways.

I placed a call on the burn out phone to Red and for the first time I broke the code no time to waste get me 20 bricks and 300K in 10 mins to the underground then hung up no explaining no nothing just high and bye either come trew or die was all on my mind I put him at fault for letting my mom's get grabbed so wasn't nothing to say.

Then I hit Baby Jay and told him to go grab the money and work and hit me when he got everything. Then I turned the tracker on to my mom's I-phone to see her direct location time was on crack and I had 20 mins to be ready with the shit or to kill and be killed. With the I-Phone tracker I put on all our phones it gave me an advantage cuz I knew where Bryce was, but he didn't' know where I was.

Club Foxy's in Orange Tx the phone was showing that address Club Foxy's was a old spot in Orange Tx that no one used no more since 2008 it was open back in 2003 as I remembered the spot it was 15 mins out from where I was in Beaumont. I made it there in like

9 mins fuck the law I was on a mash I had sent Baby-J the address to where I was going to bring the cash and drugs but to park in the projects across the street by my car when he reach the spot. I looked trew the windows to see what I could see, and I saw Bryce with my moms and two other niggas talking and setting up to make the next move. Then I hit Baby-J while I was by the back door and explained that my phone will ring in less than 5 mins to wait outside the jeep on the other side from where he park with his guns ready and for him to let Jay Jr know what to do and what's going on to bring back up to wherever I say next.

Just like clockwork my phone rang caller I.D. showed none so I knew it was go time yea I said nigga fuck you Bryce said laughing nigga you got my bread he spoke up? Say the place bitch money ant shit I shot back. Good nigga Bryce said cuz I was gone off this bitch foe the phone hung up pussy you just bought ya moms more airtime ya lil bitch Bryce started running me boiling hot. Talk to you in 15 mins bitch nigga when I tell you where to meet and drop the bread try any funny shit and I'm offing the bitch. Then Bryce hung up.

Five minutes later I'd got a text from mom's phone 2200 16th Street Orange, Tx blue house drop the bags in the trash by the road then bounce anything except that she dead! You got 30 minutes to drop and go it said.

From that text I knew the nigga was up to no good and would kill my T-jones regardless so when he would call in 15 minutes to check on it all and my wear abouts

I would tell him it's all good.

I hit Jay Jr with the address that was sent to me and told him to meet Baby Jay to make the drop.

In 15 minutes my phone rung again mom's calling it read yea I stated where my shit Bryce asked on its way nigga you got 15 minutes left then hung up I knew that meant someone would be at the house or around that house to get the work and money then hit Bryce and then he would off my mother, so I told Jay Jr leave a empty bag in the trash and meet Baby Jay all was a go from there.

Jay Jr did just like told Baby Jay parked back in the projects across from Foxy's just like before as I watched Bryce and the other two.

I sucked some gas into a bottle just to start a lil fire on the old club to get them niggas out then went back to the window on the opposite side I started the small fire. Then my phone went off it's that time bitch where my shit Bryce stated! In the trash I replied! Good bitch as he hung up noticing the fire. Damn we got to move I heard him say so I texted Baby Jay get ready its go time they coming out bet Baby Jay hit back.

Holding my T-jones by her neck with a bag on her head they pushed her out the door towards a car to the far right the fire did its trick made them niggas panic and move fast to try to get away from the closed build-ing soon as they thought it was all good and opened the back car door I popped off hitting both niggas in the back of they shit while Baby Jay and Jay Jr crept up on Bryce who tried to run and squeezed on that nigga right there while I finished the other two nigga off and grabbed ma.

Not knowing if the laws was coming or the nigga had people to back him I picked up ma and we ran back to the projects to blend in and get in our cars I put mom in with Baby J and watched them drive off before I pulled off as I took all the money and drugs in the car with me.

CHAPTER 21

The ride back to Beaumont from Orange was a long scary ride nigga had Fed money and hot guns all in the car, so I played by the rules long as the boys and ma was good I was cool with that Baby J and Jay Jr was in the jeep Baby Jay drove while Jay Jr sat in the back with his grandma. His goons drove the car. He'd come in back to Beaumont Tx with their guns and shit they played they role to the T. them young niggas was on point the whole way like true solders. We left Bryce facedown right next to the car overkill just like he earned them nigga with them I just knocked they tops off never saw them before must be them cats from Houston Bryce would run with. Crazy part it was only the start of my problems cuz soon as I made it back to Beaumont shit gone be just as real before I left. I pulled up to the Hampton Inn Rooms and got my mom a $250 room for the week at that price a night I didn't trust her at home with all the shit going down. When she got set-tled in she went in on me. Damn you son you brought all this harm on me I never wanna see you again she cried. I understood and just told her to rest to never speak on nothing she'd just been through. I left money and told Baby J to stay with her for the night. Baby J was cool with his grandma was his heart since lil and he knew not to leave her alone in times like that anyways.

Me and Jay Jr took off and headed out back to them South Park Streets. First I had to go stash the money and drugs. So I went to the house that Jaz was staying in an put all the shit in the attic locked it up then changed in some different shit all black it was from here on out.

I knew by now Zilla and his mom and sis would untie each other by this time so I didn't worry about going check that spot, but I had new plans. Big Red had to go he failed my mother and let her get taken. The money was no longer important it was a all-out war and I had to clean up and get my family safe. I called Big Red to make good on the work and money but that was the least I was gone do when he met up with me he was on high tide due to the way I'd talked on the phone, but he just asked did I get her back. Me knowing this nigga knows everything I answered yes then I pulled out on Red. Say man I told you I loved my family too and I never brought harm your way I explained but you failed me you let them niggas get to my mother you say I could trust your men now my mom is out the park for the rest of the game Red I stated looking him eye to eye. Yea son we failed and the nigga who slipped up he dead so don't betray ya family son we gone make it all ok he said to me before I squeezed and dropped Red to the ground. I know that shit was cold, and the shit hurt my soul, but I knew Red good enough soon as I'd leave I was a dead man cuz I brought the streets to Red door and that's a no when it comes to his family I knew the next step was death for me cuz Red would have anything removed that could come back on him and I wasn't ready to go.

CHAPTER 22

Leaving the underground I knew I had to get the fuck out of Beaumont and fast me and my whole family. I knew by 7:00 am the streets would be at my door looking for my head! I knew nothing was safe and it was already 6:00 am so I had to move fast.

I rushed back to the Big House where Jaz and the work and money was shit I was gone need all that wherever I stopped at. I rushed Jaz to load up the BMW 745 while I grabbed the shit I'd stashed in the attic and put all of it in the trunk while calling Baby Jay on his phone. I told Baby J to take off and head out of Texas to Louisiana and wait on me in Lake Charles after he meet up with Jay Jr.

Then I called Sunshine while on the way to her and told her to grab clothes only and be at the door in five minutes. I made it to Sunshine and as she jumped in I pulled off soon as the door closed. Ready to hit the highway knowing shit would be good long as I'd left Texas. I left Jen behind she would just be extra baggage and I ant need that. Deep down I just felt Jen wasn't made for my type of shit.

I-10 East it was all the way to Louisiana we went just as the clock struck 7:00. I called Baby Jay to see if everything was good and he let me know he was off and a little past Orange Tx. So I relaxed knowing my boys and my T-Jones would be good. I didn't have no full plan but with 300K and 20 bricks everything would be a go wherever I'd make it to and start over.

When we got towards Orange Tx there was cops everywhere on and off the freeway. Crazy thing they were checking cars for suspects in a killing and a club fire that happened earlier that night. Man my heart was in my shoe when the law walked to the car. I played it cool Hello officer how's things going I'd asked – not good he stated we got bodies everywhere been up all morning looking for suspects he stated. License and registration he asked next as I handed him my info while he looked all over the car. Where are you folks going all packed up he asked next? To see family in Lake Charles I replied back to the cop. Then he said sit tight be right back with you as he ran my info trew the system I knew I was good on that, but all the shit in the car had me on shook.

Ten minutes felt like ten hours, but he came back to the car and told me I could move on about my way. Damn that made me feel good we got back on the road as he went to the next few cars it was all good from there, so I called Baby J to see if they made it through. Yea pops my boy answered you good I asked? Yea pops we almost in Lake Charles we gone stop at the Hilton by the Casino he let me know then hung up. The cops just had waved them trew after a quick look over with them so that let me know they knew who they must be looking for older niggas at least I figured.

We made it to the room in Lake Charles around 11:00 am even and I ordered four rooms one for the boys and moms two for me and the girls and one for the work and money. We all unpacked and laid low for the rest of the night first thing in the a.m. we would be back on the move to get more deeper in Louisiana than Lake Charles so I ordered us all food and just sat back thinking on where I would start from when we settled in.

The next morning we went to Enterprise to rent a car for the drugs to ride in and I put 200K in the jeep walls of the back cargo space so if anything would happen the boys would have cash to make moves.

I put $9,000 in my pocket and stashed the rest deep in the BMW 745 trunk, while I hid the work in the rental that Sunshine would drive the rest of the way we went back to the room before we made it back we stopped at the store and gassed up the rental and the BMW 745 past full so we could drive for hours until the next fill up.

Back at the room I told everybody to get ready to move then I grabbed Baby Jay keys to the Jeep so I could go fill his shit up. I told everyone to be ready when I come back cuz we was out the door soon as.

I made it down stairs to the Jeep and started to pull out. Everything was cool until I made it to the end of the driveway a car pulled in front me and lit my shit up non stop with machine guns bullets ripped the car open I just mashed the gas and ran head into the other car but not after I was hit a few times I knew it I felt it I just couldn't stop it so I just moved on all adrenaline opened the door and ran as far as I could while the shooter's car pulled off to get away. Soon as they did Baby Jay and Jay Jr was by my side guns in hand I told them niggas to get the money out the Jeep and get back to the room and take the BMW 745 and the rental and just go as people came over to look and help then I blacked the fuck out.

CHAPTER 23

I woke up in ICU in a hospital in Lake Charles I was all alone when my eyes opened then a nurse came in she checked my I.V. cleaned me up then called the doctor in while I was just looking not able to talk with tubes in my mouth. The doctor came in and checked my vitals and ordered removal of my breathing tubes and let me breath on my own then watched the monitor to make sure all was good then they left out not telling me shit maybe cuz I couldn't say shit anyways cuz I was asking all type of shit, but nothing came out, so I knew I was down bad, so I just went to sleep.

When I woke back up I was in a different room doing much better I could feel it. To my surprise Sunshine was sitting right next to a nigga she jumped up and ran to me and kissed on me like my wife or some shit. First thing I asked was for my family and she told me that she placed them in Lafyette LA and everyone was good when they squared up she shot back to be with me say they got a nice lil house out there low key four-bedroom spot they pay rent on then I asked how long I was out she said three full weeks then the door opened and in came three cops from Lake Charles Orange and Beaumont. When I saw that I knew I was fucked how deep was the only question as they told Sunshine to leave the room which she refused until being threatened to be locked away on charges of interfering with police work and a murder investigation. I dropped my head and knew it was going to be a long ride. Man them fuck boys gave me the blues soon as Sunshine cleared the door mother fuckers was just waiting for me to come to it and wasted no time to move in on me.

I was all fucked up I'd got hit in my cheeks my arms my chest and both legs when I jumped out the truck I didn't even know if I would walk again and all they wanted to do was lock my bitch ass up.

Lawyer was all I repeated soon as the cops asked their first question. Do you know who killed Jessie Williams AKA Mr. Big Red. I was shook on that one. Why would Orange PD and Lake Charles PD be here just for a Beaumont murder? I thought to myself then the Orange Police asked did I know who killed a Bryce Floyd of Beaumont in Orange City limits. Then I knew it was more to it than I thought I just stated cool and calm lawyer please. Then laid my head back knowing this was gone be a long ride.

CHAPTER 24

Fresh out the hospital to a jail cell in Lake Charles in a wheelchair and all.

Motherfuckers put all type of charges on me I just couldn't figure how! I didn't leave shit behind nowhere. Then the lawyer Sunshine had got for me all they had was my pone calls from towers around where the murders went down. I knew the one with Big Red was a hit and miss cuz that was a burn phone he provided so nothing about that phone traced back to me they was trying voice recognition to make a conviction. With Bryce I only talked on my mom phone so they ant have no convo with us on his phone they got off but a text he sent me about a house in Orange Tx that's some good shit that a bull shit lawyer would loose too easily. I just prayed this lawyer was the real deal and for 50k he'd better be.

After stating all the facts to my lawyer and what all

they had on me I knew I would make it home just when was the only thing. No guns no fingerprints no camera footage I was good on reasonable doubt but pure facts I just would hope the jury would see trew the skims.

My boys brought my mom back to Houston Tx she wanted to be with my sisters and out our ways she ant feel none of that shit I changed her whole life all with my street bull shit.

Six months straight I stayed in Lake Charles jail waiting to be brought back to Beaumont, Tx with no bail. I started walking again but I needed a walker. My boys set up shop in Lafayette LA and had shit on Zoom man dope was twice as high in LA than in Beaumont so what went for 22K would go for 40K easy, but they let it go for 36K a brick just to stop the fuss, so my boys became the man in no time.

Jaz took care of the house shit and made the boys get in school while Sunshine took care of me and lawyers.

I woke up on chain to get flew into Beaumont Jefferson County Jail to wait my trial day out, which would be another six month to a year then I would have to go to Orange to do the same shit when that was done.

I know it would be two or more years before I made it back out, but I didn't' trip I had 9gs on my books my boys at it 100% and Sunshine on every play I needed done I just knew being back in Beaumont shit was gone get real.

I had to get my strength back right and fast I felt the smoke coming so I sharpened a fork and made a knife just in case a nigga tried me while I was weak.

Shit hit the fan four weeks later in Jefferson County Jail while I was in the shower. Three niggas came at me talking shit about the last niggas I expected the nigga Duck! Them niggas acted all hard and shit talking all crooked and shit till I hit the first bitch nigga right in his shit flushed him and charged the next two up. Niggas saw that and jumped on dick fast and rode down with me. It was cool cuz I ant wanna catch no body while on trial for one. I knew I needed to get out that bitch fast. That was just the start of the shit I knew more shit would come. The streets was talking, and shit all pointed to me so I couldn't even sleep in that bitch.

Next week it was some more shit nigga called me out over some North side South side shit say the South the reason they Big Homie E was dead I guess my brother stayed solid and kept shit in the street cuz I ant hear shit about E-Body or K-Dug or the nigga B.M. So I knew that smoke would come soon too. Me and them niggas from the North had it out full fledge on the courtyard few niggas rode with me cuz I wasn't 100% but rode like I was.

The guards moved me to max wing M-Dorm they called it say I had too much shit going on since I'd been in the county. Nigga started sending death threats and shit while I was back on M-Dorm, so I called for Baby Jay and Jay Jr to slide back home and touch some niggas people since they wanted to play threats with my life I got niggas girls beat up bad niggas dogs killed just dumb shit I didn't catch no bodies though just sent messages back letting niggas know it was real.

The next five months came by, and I was up for trial shit lasted two full weeks man I can't lie I thought I'd lost the D.A. showed shit I didn't even remember but nothing put me with the body the phone call wasn't clear to match my voice with and no solid evidence, so my lawyer did her best shit and got me off the Big Red shit a year later.

Now I got to sit in Orange County since that's where Bryce body was. That shit was trash but better than Beaumont county due to less problems. I even got some pussy in Orange County from a C.O. named DeDe. A nice lil yella from Orange Tx fell for a nigga say I was just different to her. She dropped cigarettes to me every three days and fucked me every other night she would call me out to work and let me hit in the closet so that all passed that time a lil faster I'd been gone for a year and six months waiting to go to trail for Bryce in two months. I used that time to work out and get back right so I could get back to it when I made it out.

Two months came and shit got real Orange County Courts ant play the move my lawyer batted shit down the more shit they brought up shit ant look good at all I almost asked for a deal, but I stayed strong all they had was a text and an address that ant nothing happen at, so I let my lawyer work three weeks and it was over all charges dropped.

I would be a free man in 24 hours Sunshine was there

the whole fucking way. I would never forget that shit not one bit.

The next day around 1:00 the doors opened to let me go free the news was there and doing a story on the change of events. My boys was there in some new shit new cars new everything Jaz was there and my star Sunshine.

Lil did I know some other people was there too real close by. Look like a good day for me for the most part at least.

CHAPTER 25

We left the county and headed back towards Louisiana to get to the new stomping grounds. I asked my boys if they was strapped and like clockwork they both pulled out I grabbed me a nice 9mm from Jay Jr and sat it on my lap some shit just didn't feel right so we took off no looking back I was glad that part was dead now just had to face the rest.

We made it to a town name Buna and had to get some gas and shit everything was clear, and we was all taking care of shit then a car pulled up to the pump next to us. Thinking nothing of it when a pretty female stepped out to go in to the store while Jay Jr pumped the gas I counted the lil money Sunshine handed me while Baby Jay checked his music list something just told me to look up and when I did I saw Zilla getting out the back seat pistol in hand while the broad that went in the store held a gun standing at the front to the car she got out all I could think of was Jay Jr and how he was hit I bussed trew the car glass jumping out with out saying shit and just in time cuz Zilla hit Jay Jr right in the chest. As he fell back Baby Jay popped the female in her top and knocked her dead flat.

Zilla crawled to the other side of his car with someone else jumped out shooting from the driver seat shit was on and guns was going off.

Jay Jr was in bad shape I could tell, and my anger got the best of me I went Rambo cuz I didn't want no other shots to hit my nigga shit lasted for like five full minutes then I heard sirens I helped put Jay Jr in the back seat while Sunshine took the wheel I told them to burn off while me and Baby Jay stayed behind. M y own fucking blood is the only blood that I keep shedding I said in my head I hit my brother baby momma he hit my son I shot my brother and killed my plug how did it get to this then bamb one hit my arm and dropped me it was live or die so Baby Jay put in work and hit the nigga who got out the driver seat twice in the chest.

It was just me and Zilla ready to shoot to the death when I saw Sunshine pull of safe I went back in bitch nigga you gone die I told Zilla. Nigga I been dead fuck you he said back while me and Baby Jay locked eyes hey go left I go right to corner Zilla in the nigga hit me again in my leg and dropped me while Baby Jay hit him from the blind and knocked Zilla top off.

The sirens got closer so I knew it was over I took

Baby Jay gun and told him to take Zilla car and go as he left the laws pulled in and ran to the people on the ground I knew I would get life for this shit no way around it three hours after beating a murder case.

I just laid back and passed out!!

✦ 114 ✦

To be continued in Book Two
Coming Soon!